IMMORTAL BEINGS

M.D.

authorHOUSE®

AuthorHouse™
1663 Liberty Drive
Bloomington, IN 47403
www.authorhouse.com
Phone: 1 (800) 839-8640

Published by AuthorHouse 10/12/2018

ISBN: 978-1-5462-6446-0 (sc)
ISBN: 978-1-5462-6445-3 (hc)
ISBN: 978-1-5462-6444-6 (e)

Library of Congress Control Number: 2018912326

AUTHOR'S ACKNOWLEDGEMENT

This book is dedicated to my family and friends. I love you all. To my unconditionally loving, supportive mother. Thank you for always being there, for believing in me, and encouraging me to dream big. To my brother whom I love and support. Thank you for your sibling ship. To all my friends who are wonderful, inspiring, and have been there for me. Thank you for your friendship. To all the positive, influential people in my life. I appreciate all of you. Thank you for everything.

PART ONE

CHAPTER ONE

It was a chaotic Thursday morning. The day began with the alarm failing to wake me up. My six-foot-tall, athletic, brown-eyed, long purple haired roommate, Kayla took the liberty to stall in the shower in our single bathroom dormitory. I felt my bladder was going to explode by the time she finished.

"Finally!" I exclaimed when she walked out of the bathroom.

"Okay, Sake. It's all yours," sneered Kayla. Kayla and I didn't get along very well. She disliked how much stuff I had. My belongings consisted of five large sport bags and three gigantic boxes. I moved into the dorm a week ago and still needed to finish unpacking. I didn't like how untidy and inconsiderate she was.

"The name's Sakura." I told her bitterly. Kayla enjoyed teasing me.

"Oh? Is it?"

"Yes." I said firmly.

"Okay girly, whatever you say," she replied obnoxiously. She bent over to lean into my face and forced an unpleasant smile. Her two front teeth were gone, and her breath smelled like garlic. I winced, hurried to the bathroom, and prepared for school.

I pedaled as fast as I could on my green mountain bike. My legs cramped as I felt circulating blood rush up and down my legs. A red mustang sped by me, almost hitting my back tire.

"Stupid driver. Watch the damn road." I muttered to myself. It was raining hard that morning and my clothes were completely soaked. Drops of rain dribbled down from my helmet and landed on my nose. I shook my head every few minutes so that the raindrops wouldn't interfere with my navigation. I lived in a city called Sea Town, and it often rained. I wished it were a dry morning and that I woke up earlier.

After arriving to school, I parked my bike and started running to my classroom. University of Washeendom State had a large campus. As I ran to class I could hear nothing more than the drumming of raindrops, my rapid heartbeat, and the thumping of my feet.

"Great." I thought sarcastically. *"This is just brilliant! I can't believe I'm late on the first day in college! Luckily, I just have this one psychology class today."* Gritting my teeth, I broke into a sprint. My back ached from my heavy backpack. My lungs felt as if they would burst any moment. I ran with caution, because the cement was slippery.

I finally reached the classroom. I swung the door wide open. Trying to halt myself from running any further, I slipped on the linoleum floor. I fell flat on my face, unconscious.

I dreamt a realistic, yet bizarre scenario where I was being chased by a ferocious, angry canine figure. It growled and tried to fiercely bite me. I was in a dark, remote forest where not a single human being lived within several miles. My heartbeat increased exponentially with great intensity. The pain in my legs made me want to stop running. Despite the pain and sudden cramps, I continued to endure. I kept running for my life. Unfortunately, I was unable to see the large a few feet away from me. I tripped on the rock and fell flat on my face on to the wet, dirt filled ground. I could hear the dog's growling just a few yards away. I was terrified. I felt I had no choice but to surrender.

Suddenly, someone in a black cloak appeared in front of me like magic. This stealthy person hovered above the beast and landed on top of the creature by surprise. The figure and canine wrestled briefly until the dog lost all energy. The canine collapsed at the end of the brawl and yelped helplessly. The individual's head was buried in its neck, devouring it. I wanted to scream or vomit, but my mouth was completely dry. I was too scared to even shriek. The inexplicable figure looked up at me, its mouth covered with blood from the canine, and its eyes glowed yellow.

"Wake up, sleepy head." whispered a voice in my ear. I recognized it belonged to a woman, but I didn't know who she was. I opened my eyelids and saw here. I laid on a back on a comfortable large bed. She sat beside me at the edge of the bed. She was young, attractive, and appeared to be in her mid-twenties. Her eyes sparkled sky blue. They were bright and very blue.

Her complexion was clear, vanilla, and milky. She had shiny, long, straight dark red hair that almost looked brunette. Her figure was fit and slender.

"Are you feeling okay? You had quite a hard fall," she said. She spoke with genuine concern. Her voice was soft spoken like when a mother cradles and sooths her child to sleep. It sounded sweet, gentle, and mellow.

I opened my mouth to say, "Yes," but no sound came out. I found myself too nervous and shy to speak to such a stunning stranger. Instead, I nodded. The woman giggled. She tossed her lovely hair away from her face.

"It looks to me that you aren't in the mood to speak," she stated observantly. Feeling a bit awkward, I cleared my throat.

"What happened? And how did I get here?" I asked. My true initial question I had in mind was, "Who are you and why are you so beautiful?" However, such inquiries weren't ones I would ask right after meeting a person.

I scanned my surroundings. The bedroom was very spacious. Five yards away was a mahogany table where there was a desktop computer. A comfortable office chair was barely a foot away from the table. There was a massive wardrobe next to the door. I noticed a bathroom nearby. A large television set was conveniently situated across the bed. A stereo was next to the grandfather clock that near the door. The walls were painted light blue. The bed I was lying on was a luxury. It was king sized and very comfortable. Next to the bed were three sets of windows with opened blinds in which sunshine came into the room, illuminating it. It was a beautiful sight and lovely bedroom. I wished the room were my own.

"*Wow!*" I thought. "*What a room! This is a lot better than back home.*" My bedroom at home was small, cramped, and stuffy. The bed was stiff as a board and the walls were white and bare.

"Well," the woman began, "You did save my life, you know."

I stared at her with a blank expression, baffled.

"I did?" I asked. I wasn't convinced by the news at all.

"Yes," she said firmly.

"Why do you say that?" I questioned, wondering how in the world I could have done anything heroic.

"You don't remember?" She didn't seem convinced by my response.

"I guess not." I admitted, perplexed.

"Well," she began. She explained the entire event to me.

The woman was in a rush to get to class this morning. As she ran up the staircase that led to the school entrance, she slipped and fell backwards. According to her, I caught her before she collapsed onto the ground. She wanted to thank me, but I was already sprinting yards away. She ran after me and witnessed me fall when I got to class. She rushed over and intervened to help. She took me to her car and drove me to her house to nurse me back to proper health. I told her the entire tale was vague in my memory and agreed that I had a really hard fall.

"Thank you for taking good care of me all this time." I said. I felt myself becoming flushed when I said this. I did feel grateful for her kind deed, though.

"And thank you for catching me when I fell. I could have suffered a major injury, you know." She smiled. I noticed two small dimples formed. Her smile made me smile as well. Suddenly, I felt a pang of embarrassment.

"Was I heavy? You did carry me to your car, right?" I asked. I had to know because I felt guilty.

"A nice student in the class offered to carry you to my car. But I did carry you to the house. You were as light as a feather. Don't worry about it." She replied casually.

"Oh, how generous of that person." I was referring to the student. "I wish I could have said thank you."

"No worries. I did that for the both of us." she said in a reassuring manner and added, "The student who helped was named Robby Samson."

There was an awkward silence that followed. It lasted only a few seconds, but I felt it was longer. Before I knew it, the woman was introducing herself.

"My name's Jenna. Jenna Watson." She extended her hand to me.

"Nice to meet you, Jenna. I'm Sakura. Sakura Hatsukawa." I stretched my arm out to shake her hand. Her fingers were slender and defined with long, manicured nails that were covered with lavender nail polish. Her hand was also soft and smooth.

"Likewise. I'm assuming you're Japanese. I like your name. What does it mean?"

"Thank you. And yes, I'm Japanese. I am half Japanese, a quarter Filipina, and a quarter Spanish. My name means cherry blossom"

"Wow. That's an interesting mix. Cherry blossoms are pretty flowers. I like them. Can you speak the languages?" I could tell Jenna was impressed.

"Yes. But I'm not fluent. I lack the most in Spanish, but I'm more capable of communicating in both Japanese and Tagalog."

"Hontou desuka? Ja, watashiwa Asutereriajin to Inugurandojin desu." ("Really? Well, I'm Australian and English.")

I broke out laughing. "I don't think you pronounced neither Australian nor English correctly in Japanese." Jenna laughed, too. She added she had New Zealander in her heritage, too.

"I have both accents of mainly English and Australian. I use them interchangeably." She said.

"Interesting. How did you learn Japanese?" I asked, intrigued.

"I took three years of it in high school, and it sort of stuck with me. I'm not fluent, but I remember a few phrases."

"Impressive." When I said this, Jenna blushed.

"Tondemonai." she snorted in Japanese. ("Far from it.")

I couldn't help but smile. Jenna became my first friend in college. Little did I expect how far our relationship would go, for we bonded very quickly.

CHAPTER TWO

I stirred in my sleep. I was dreaming being involvement in a potential crime where I˙was chased by two people who tried to kidnap me for ransom. Before I could scream, I woke up, sweating, but relieved. I rolled over on to my side and tried to fall asleep again. The next time I woke up, I was lying on the wooden floor next to my bed. I moved in my sleep and fell off my bed. I lifted my head and glanced at the grandfather clock near the door. It was a quarter before eight in the morning, and I had fifteen minutes to get to psychology class.

"Oh shitty!" I exclaimed aloud. Suddenly, my cell phone rang. I grabbed my pink purse and retrieved it.

"Hello?" I said.

"Good morning my sweet daughter." It was my mum, Elizabeth Smart.

"Hi mum."

"Jenna, it's the first day of school, isn't it?"

"Yes, mum. I can't talk right now. I'm going to arrive late." I said quickly.

"Oh. Okay, sweetie. Be good and take care. I'll give you call another time. I love you."

"Love you too, mum." I hung up.

I fled to the bathroom where I washed my face and brushed my teeth. I grabbed a hairbrush and frantically brushed my long, dark red hair that looked almost brunette. Afterwards, I jumped into the shower and rushed to get clean. Then I ran to my wardrobe in my bath towel, which slipped off. I stood naked, frantically searching for an outfit. There wasn't much time remaining, and I didn't care what I wore. I left the house and hopped into my red mustang in black slacks, a blue tank top, and gray sandals.

I had no time to put makeup on. I did not expect to come to school late that day.

I arrived at school that Thursday morning ten minutes tardy. Most of it was due to horrendous traffic congestion. During the commute I turned the radio on and listened to today's forecast.

"Good morning, Sea Town. Thank you for joining us on Pacific Northwest Highlighting News on the radio. I'm Monte Jackson, your meteorologist for today. This morning is extremely foggy. Temperatures are approximately in the mid-forties. Be careful when you drive. Remember to keep those car lights on. The high today is sixty-eight degrees Fahrenheit. Tonight's low is going to be fifty-three degrees. It will rain later this afternoon, so be sure to have those umbrellas with you. Furthermore, there's a chance of a thunderstorm, which won't occur until very late tonight…" I turned the radio off and changed the station to listen to music instead.

I sped by a young, Asian looking woman who arrived by bicycle. As I ran up the staircase to the entrance of my school, I slipped on the wet ground. I felt myself falling backwards, doomed to be more than ten minutes late. To my surprise, I felt a pair of strong arms catch me. I turned my head and it was the Asian looking woman I saw earlier. She looked flustered and in a hurry. Grinning, she sprinted off before I could say anything.

"Wait!" I said, but she was too far to hear me.

I ran after her. My knees started to ache. I have not run this intense in a long while. By the time I caught up with her, she was face down in the classroom I was in, too. I hurried and kneeled next to the woman. I placed two fingers on to her throat, slightly pressing to check if she had a pulse. I was extremely relieved she was still breathing. She was passed out and was going to be okay.

The professor was Mr. Richard. He was an old, disheveled, hotheaded, fragile man. He was shocked by the abrupt interruption. His face turned from pasty white to beet red within a second.

"Get out!" he hollered in a deep, booming voice. "A class is in session!"

I was about to protest that someone was hurt, but he didn't notice at all. Before I could pick up the woman, a student volunteered to carry her out. He insisted that we take her to the hospital, but I refused. I told him that I worked part time as a nurse and assured him that all she needed was to rest. He believed my falsehood and he allowed me to handle the situation. I drove towards home again, thankful that the traffic wasn't a hassle. It was just that one psychology class I had for the day, and I did not feel guilty missing class this one time. My focus was helping this woman get back to good health.

CHAPTER THREE

I woke up the next day in Jenna's bed to lavender fragrance. It was a nice way to rise in the morning. Jenna spent the night sleeping on the sofa downstairs. I was still dressed in my navy-blue jeans and green t-shirt I wore yesterday. Glimpsing at the grandfather clock, it read six a.m. Class started in two hours. I crawled out of bed and walked downstairs. The house was two stories high and very tidy. The wooden floors and clean, white walls added elegance, which made the home cozier and more luxurious. The staircase led to the living room, where a fireplace and large, cushioned, green sofa was situated. A massive home theater television set with big stereo speakers stood in front of the couch.

I entered the dining room. In the center was a long, rectangular, mahogany table for ten people. A classy chandelier hung above it. Four large mirrors surrounded the room, two on each wall. There was a gigantic, sleek, wooden case that held various, fancy table wear. It displayed wineglasses, plates, bowls, china, and tea sets. Not too far away was the smell of toasted bread and fruit. I could hear someone humming a lullaby. It was Jenna.

I walked into the kitchen and found her wearing a pretty, black dress and white high heels. She had a blue apron on, too. I could tell that without the heels, her height was about five foot seven inches. I thought she looked lovely in her outfit.

"Well, good morning, Sakura." she said cheerfully. She was cooking waffles and preparing fruit. The cooking of waffles plus the fruit sent an intoxicating aroma in the air. I sniffed the scent more, and my stomach rumbled loudly. Jenna heard it. She laughed. "Looks like someone's hungry." She turned her head and smiled at me.

"Good morning." I said and stretched my arms. I thanked her making breakfast. I felt stiff. "Need a hand?"

"Oh no, no, no. You're the guest, Sakura. Thank you for the offer though. Why don't you go shower, and then have breakfast with me? Then, I'll drive us to school."

"Okay, thanks." I felt like she was treating me like a child. *"I'm older than I look,"* I thought. People mistaken me to be fifteen or a year younger than that, but I was nineteen and turning twenty very soon. "Where's the nearest bathroom?" I asked.

"There's one in the living room, near the door." I thanked her again and strolled out to wash up.

CHAPTER FOUR

Within ten minutes of inconspicuous speeding, I finally reached my house. The building was two stories high and painted baby blue on the outside. I carried the Asian looking woman like an oversize child. One arm was under her head and the other under her knees. I recalled leaving the front door unlocked, so I kicked it open and ran upstairs to the bedroom. I laid her down on my bed and examined her forehead, gently touching the bump. A small stream of blood began trickling out of it. Suddenly, I felt weak. My stomach grumbled, and my throat became dry. I felt famished and thirsty, but I knew I had to care for the woman before I could concentrate on myself. Immediately, I grabbed a damp towel and wiped her head clean. When the bleeding ceased, I placed an ice pack on it.

I sat quietly beside her on the edge of the bed. Half of the time I was staring at her, and at my lavender polished fingernails. I was unaware of how much time passed. I took some time to look at the woman thoroughly. I thought she was pretty and obviously young. Her hair was long, black and thick. I ran my fingers through her hair, and realized it was soft, too. She had a small, but rather cute nose that suited her oval face. Her complexion was light brown and like a mocha pigment. I was taller than her, but not by much. She was about five foot three inches and possessed an athletic figure. Her arms were visibly toned, and I was certain that this was the case for the rest of her body.

I removed the ice pack and leaned forward to her face to examine the bump. Fortunately, it was healing quickly. My palm involuntarily rested on her right cheek. I caressed it, enjoying its softness and warmth. The tip of my fingers slid down her neck. It was slender and silky. An urge to nibble on it arose, but I refrained myself from such temptation. For someone I didn't know, nor haven't met, I felt a mysterious vibe from this woman.

She was gorgeous, yes, and I couldn't help but feel attracted to her. Her lips were small but felt smooth and warm when I touched them with my fingertip. I kissed them, only for a few seconds and got a tingly sensation from it. I wisely desisted going any further.

Suddenly, she slowly tossed her head and gently moved her legs under the sheets. A smile formed on my face as I whispered in her ear, "Wake up, sleepy head."

CHAPTER FIVE

After I showered, I looked at myself in the mirror. I noticed a small bump on the center of my forehead. Fortunately, my bangs would conceal it. I left the bathroom, feeling crisp and neat, despite the old clothes I wore. I wished I could have changed my undergarments, too.

I joined Jenna in the dining room. We sat across from one another, but within earshot. There were two plates with a Belgium waffle and a side of fruit – pineapple, grapes, blueberries, and apple slices, along with a purple pitcher filled with orange juice. A small vase with blue roses in it served as a centerpiece. My plate was the only plate with a small side of Canadian Bacon.

"Are you vegetarian?" I questioned. Jenna nodded.

"I thought you might like it after ordering that pizza last night." Jenna commented.

"Oh, thanks. You're very observant."

"You're welcome. So are you." We both smiled at each other.

The breakfast food was delicious. I thanked Jenna for cooking and told her she was a good a cook. She thanked me with a big, warm smile.

We ate our meal in silence, which bothered me because I was used to speaking during mealtimes. I didn't know what to say after thanking her for the meal. When I came up with something, I thought it was a dull, redundant subject. I also felt rude because I had terrible posture as I ate. My back slouched, and both my elbows were on the table. On the contrary, Jenna sat erect, one arm on her lap as the other one handled the food.

"She must think I come from a crude family." I thought, irritated at myself.

I offered to wash the dishes when I was done, but she told me not to worry. She directed I place them all in the dishwasher. Dishwashers are convenient, but to an extent. I could never trust them to thoroughly clean my kitchenware. I once became ill after drinking a dirty glass that was just washed. I did what she told me to do anyway. After cleaning up we both gathered our school supplies and drove to school.

CHAPTER SIX

"I'm hungry. Want to order food?" I rubbed my belly. "Can I get you anything to drink? I am thirsty."

"No thank you, Jenna. Can we have pizza?"

"Absolutely. Good idea, Sakura. I'm going downstairs to get water. Come with me. We'll order pizza." I stood up and left the room. Sakura got out of bed and followed me to the kitchen.

"Do you live here alone?" she asked.

"Yes. It used to belong to my aunt. She passed away a few years ago, and I ended up inheriting this house and her financial sources. She was a rich, classy, business woman who worked closely with Microsoft. She was also vice president of Boeing. I was her only niece and closest relative. So, she left everything she had to me."

"I see. It's very quiet here," she stated bluntly. "Do you get lonely?"

"Not really. There are a lot of good memories I have here with my aunt. So, it keeps me somewhat content. But I do get lonesome. That's what going out is for." I changed the subject. "What toppings do you want on your pizza?"

"Canadian bacon and pineapple, please."

"Okay." I picked up the phone receiver, dialed the number for Pizza Shack, and ordered one large pizza that was half Canadian bacon and half cheese.

Within ten minutes, the pizza man arrived. To my surprise, the pizza man was Robby Samson from psychology class. He was the person who helped me carry Sakura to my car earlier that day.

"Robby Samson?" I said.

"Well, if it isn't Miss Jenna Watson," he said and smiled broadly at me. Robby had green eyes and short, golden blonde hair with bangs that covered his forehead. His body was lean and athletic.

"Thanks for the pizza." I said.

"You're welcome. Is anyone home with you now?"

"Yes. I have a guest."

"Oh? That's too bad." Robby frowned.

"Why?"

"Being the pizza man isn't the only thing I do, if you know what I mean. Especially when I deliver to beautiful women," said Robby. He winked at me.

"What are you implying?" I asked suspiciously.

"Oh, nothing," he said quickly. Then he added with a flirtatious, yet serious tone, "I was about to ask you if you wanted some company tonight. Perhaps someone to share your pizza with? I can be exceptional company. I can help satisfy any hunger needs you have in and out of bed. All you have to do is say yes and let me in."

"You're such a flirt." I teased.

"Oh? I already know that," boasted Robby. He leaned closer to my face. I leaned back, away from his face.

"Just so you know. The answer to the advancements you just made to me is a no. Not just for now. Not ever. The answer will always be no. Stop wasting your time and don't ask me again. I'm not interested." I said with firmness and a serious tone. Robby's eyes widened. He appeared shock and in disbelief.

"Here, this is my payment in cash. Now leave. Keep the change. Have a good night." I paid for the order and quickly shut the door before Robby could say anything else. Sakura and I sat on the sofa in the living room as we ate and watched the Symsons.

"Do you like this show?" she asked.

"Yes. Sometimes I watch it because it's funny."

"I haven't seen this cartoon in ages. The humor is crude at times. Overall, interesting and entertaining to watch."

"Ture. I find it hilarious. I grew up watching this show," I explained. "What character do you like? I like Homen. His character is a great example of a dimwitted person who doesn't know the vast range of stupidity he possesses. And that he comes off as quite comical."

"True." she agreed. "I like Dart. He is funny, too. And clever. I like the pranks he does, and the way he instigates Homen. I like Leena, too. Although I sometimes feel sorry for her because she's the genius misfit. Margaret is very nice. She's the responsible, supportive wife and mother."

"What about Molly, the baby?" I asked.

"She's just there, playing as the toddler in the family. She's clever and intelligent, too." I nodded my head in agreement and took a bite of my slice of cheese pizza.

"Do you want wine?" I offered. "I have some in the fridge." I felt thirsty again.

"No thank you. I will take water with ice, please. I don't drink. Thanks for offering, though." Sakura smiled.

"Okay. Why don't you drink?"

"I'm not interested. I tried alcohol before and I don't like the taste. I also don't like how it makes me feel loopy. I like being sober, and I don't take anything substance wise. I'm fine without it, thank you." I looked at her young face and lifted an eyebrow.

"Okay. That is wise, and I respect that. Water it is. Also, aren't you still a minor? Even if you do drink you can't be drinking until you're twenty-one, you know." I teased.

"Well, I am twenty. Soon I am turning twenty-one, and isn't that close to the legal drinking age anyway? As you know now it's not like I'm going to get drunk and go wild." she remarked. I giggled and turned to the kitchen. I came back with one wineglass filled with red wine for myself and another glass with iced water for Sakura. We had a toast to a lovely evening.

CHAPTER SEVEN

Jenna's car smelled strongly of leather and rubber. I reckoned it was brand new. I asked if it was, and I was right. She drove with confidence and was well focused on the road.

"Yes. I bought it a week ago. Do you like it? I picked it out myself."

"Yeah. It's nice." I felt a little jealous because I didn't have a car and I couldn't drive.

"Don't you own a bike?" she asked.

"How do you know that?" I felt suspicious when she asked. I haven't mentioned to her that I commuted by bicycle.

Jenna turned her head momentarily at me and whispered hoarsely into my ear while we stopped at a red light, "I am psychic, you know." Then she winked. I broke out laughing.

"You're silly." I said, "So how did you really know?"

"I saw you riding on your bicycle the other day when I was driving to school. It was really raining hard. I'm impressed you even biked to school in such weather conditions."

"Well, I can't drive. Biking to places is environmentally friendly. Also, a nice workout."

"Why don't you drive? I like your reasons for biking."

"I haven't learned yet. I am interested. Just so I can drive if ever I need to. For now, I'm sticking with my bicycle."

"Okay. How about this - I'll teach you how to drive. You can learn on my new car. Driving a mustang feels invigorating, in my opinion. I'll teach you and help you get your driver's license if you want. You may not get a car after you get your license, but at least you know how to operate one. What do you think?"

"Really?" I asked in disbelief. No one has ever offered to teach me how to drive. I asked, "Have you ever taught anyone how to drive?"

"No. You'll be my first. Don't worry, I can be a good teacher. Give me a try. If you don't like my teaching style, you can get lessons elsewhere." Jenna smiled and winked. I felt so thankful for her proposal and willingness. I also didn't want this to be free of charge. I wanted to give something back in return for her thoughtfulness.

"Jenna, I really appreciate this. Yes, I accept your driving lessons. But not for free. There's got to be a way I can pay you, or return the favor? Because it will take some time for me to learn and be an independent driver."

"Who said anything about pay? Don't worry about that. I'll teach you. No strings attached. I remember how it was for me when before I started driving. It was my aunt who taught me. Let's just say it's my way of paying it forward. Maybe good karma will come around, too. Besides, I don't mind spending more time with you."

I blushed. I couldn't help it. Jenna had a charm about her. I replied, "Thanks. You're sweet. I wouldn't mind spending more time with you, too. Do you drink coffee?"

"Of course. We're living in a city that's good for that. Sea Town is well known for its coffee. And all the Starcash coffee shops. Why do you ask?"

"Well, I can treat you to coffee after each lesson. It's the least I can do."

"You've got yourself a deal, sugar. One grande chai tea latte after each lesson it is." Jenna winked and smiled.

"Thanks again, Jenna." I grinned.

"My pleasure, mate. Anytime." She spoke in an Australian accent. I giggled, surprised by how different she sounded. "Well, dearest, I'm about to suggest something. You can say whatever you feel about it. I am okay with whatever your stance is."

"What is it?" I asked curiously.

"I want to let you know that you can come and stay at my place, if you like. You live in a dorm, don't you? How is that coming along? If you want to you can come and live with me. It's easier that way. You and I can just split the cost of the monthly bills." That time, Jenna spoke in a distinct British accent. I liked it very much.

"I'm very flattered." I said, "Living in the dorm is okay. Not ideal for me at this point to be honest, but tolerable so far. Plus, I don't want to be a hassle, Jenna. I don't want to perturb."

"No. It's absolutely fine. In fact, I love your company, and I wouldn't be lonesome if you stayed. Will you consider it?" She seemed sincere about it. I thought about the cramped dorm and my roommate, Kayla whom I didn't get along with. I thought about how uncomfortable my bed was and the dorm bedroom being too cold. The idea of living with Jenna, whom I met recently but already felt very comfortable and got along well with felt desirable. I needed some time to think about it.

"Okay, I'll let you know soon."

"Alright." Jenna smiled.

CHAPTER EIGHT

I was happy that Sakura was in my first class. Mr. Richard didn't seem to know we existed and didn't bother to discuss with us about yesterday's incident. Sakura and I sat next to each other. Our seats were in the back of the classroom. Robby Samson waved at us from his seat that was closer to the front of the room. Sakura seemed confused but waved anyway. I didn't wave back.

It was a long, annoying hour of constant lecture. Mr. Richard's voice was so cavernous and loud that he almost bellowed whenever he spoke. I should have brought earplugs. I came equipped with a pen and paper and took notes. Sakura, on the other hand, brought a tape recorder and a separate notebook for the subject. Her hand looked as if it was scribbling on the notebook page as she keenly listened to the professor simultaneously. I noticed that she even had highlighters of various colors. Surprised by the number of objects she brought, I thought maybe I shouldn't bring anything next time and just rely on getting my supplies from her. She seemed to be the kind of student who was always prepared, attentive, and absorbed information like a sponge. For me, I like to keep my school bag light and materials minimal. I try to pay attention in class.

During the lesson, Mr. Richard asked a question that I thought didn't suit the course of Introduction to Psychology. Our lecture today was on theories in psychology.

"Why do we bother to live if we end up dying in the end? Anyone have an idea?" He asked with much curiosity in his voice. Sally Field, a small, petite woman with long, braided, brown hair raised her hand. Her voice was squeaky like a mouse.

"How does this relate to the subject of memory, Mr. Richard? Isn't that question more philosophical? I thought were just talking about behaviorism?" asked Sally. Mr. Richard's face became extremely crinkled that his skin sagged. He appeared upset.

"*Gross.*" I thought.

"Excuse me, young lady? I believe I'm the teacher here, not you. If you wish to not be a part of the class discussion, then leave! Don't come here wasting my time." He stomped his foot. Robby stood up and took defense for Sally.

"Mr. Richard, I think Sally's question was very appropriate. This is a psychology class and we were just talking about behaviorism. Nothing even close to existentialism or philosophical questioning." Robby was a good speaker. I wouldn't be surprised if he ran for politician. Two other men named Fred Little and Jack Johnson stood up and nodded in support of Robby. Fred was large and bulky-looking as a rock with long, frizzled green hair. Jack was a slender, short man with a blue Mohawk.

"I concur!" both men boomed in unison. Sally smiled and seemed a bit flattered by her group of supporters.

"Shut up! All of you! If you don't want to be here, then leave! I don't have time to deal with childish rubbish!" yelled Mr. Richard. His face turned beet red with fury. The classroom became dead silent. Robby stood up and left. Sally, Fred, and Jack followed him out the door. I felt like leaving, too, but Sakura stayed glued to her seat. Mr. Richard resumed the remaining forty minutes of class lecturing about the reproduction of various sea animals. Sakura didn't bother to take notes. She turned off her tape recorder and placed it in her backpack. Then she started reading from the psychology textbook and took notes from it. I sat there in a trance, bored out of my mind.

After class, Sakura and I walked side by side. I asked her if she was taking other classes. She said she was taking sociology and chemistry. In addition, she taught a martial arts class on campus. She had an upcoming lesson today. My jaw dropped.

"You know martial arts? What kind?"

"I know taekwondo, jujitsu, kendo, kung-fu, karate, judo, and Tai chi. My father was an instructor for an academy in Japan and he taught me all the techniques when I was very young."

"Wow, that's really cool. You should teach me sometime."

"Why don't you attend the classes? They're not too expense. I am a very effective sensei."

"I'm sorry. I can't. I work for a banking corporation. I'm an executive manager and consultant."

"I bet it pays well, though."

"It does. Very well." I smiled broadly.

"What class do you have next?" she asked.

"Accounting." I responded.

"I'm sure you'll do a fine job in that class, being an executive in financial business." she said.

"Oh yeah, you betcha." I agreed. She giggled. Her laughter makes me smile.

"Okay. I must go. Where should we meet?" she asked.

"How about I pick you up at the main entrance after your martial arts class?"

"Okay. I'll see you then. Bye." She waved at me and started walking away. I waved back.

"Ta ta." I said and watched her walk off.

CHAPTER NINE

When Jenna was out of site, I went back to the classroom to talk with Mr. Richard. The man was a bit intimidating and unapproachable at first, but I gathered enough courage to confront him. He was at the whiteboard, drawing pictures of trees and dogs.

"Did I miss any work yesterday Mr. Richard?" He looked to me, confused.

"Do I know you, young lady? And it's Friday, right?" I became nervous.

"I'm Sakura Hatsukawa. Sir, I was just in your Introduction to Psychology class last period. I sat at the back with Jenna Watson. And yes, today is Friday, sir." He muttered something that I couldn't hear.

"Excuse me?" I said.

"I said you damn Japs! How dare you bomb us at Pearl Harbor! You fucking killed my brother, Stan. He was in the military and I was back home as a civilian who couldn't save him!" He yelled at my face, his bony cheeks glowed red and his eyes widened. I wanted to run away, but I couldn't move a muscle. I was flabbergasted. He asked me, "Well, aren't you going to make amends for his death?" I shook my head.

"You're mistaken Mr. Richard. I wasn't responsible for the bombing. I had nothing to do with it. Sure, part of my family is Japanese, but I am American, sir. I grew up here and this is my home. Besides, that's in the past. We must concentrate on the present and the future. The US's diplomatic relationship with Japan has positively progressed through the years. I am sorry though about your brother, sir." I said this as calmly as I possibly could without indicating that I was terrified.

"You damn Jap! I hate 'em all. Go back to Japan where you belong!" He turned his back and continued drawing on the board. This time, he drew two men, one holding the American flag and the other a Japanese flag. He drew a large X sign over the person holding the Japanese flag.

"Goodbye, Mr. Richard." I said. I slowly walked backwards towards the door. Before I turned around to open the door, Mr. Richard threw a rock at my direction. It flew and hit my left eye.

"Never again, Japan!" he proclaimed. I hurried as fast as I could to my martial arts class. As I ran to class I received a text from my roommate, Kayla. She texted that we weren't a good roommate match and suggested that I move out. She reminded me that her family members oversee the dorm roommate assignment process and support this decision. She declared a new roommate will replace me in a few days.

CHAPTER TEN

After my accounting class I headed back to the main entrance. I arrived ten minutes late. Sakura was sitting at the staircase, patiently waiting. She was reading her notes and was wearing large, black sunglasses.

"Why are you wearing those?" I pointed at the sunglasses. "It's going to pour soon. You know how Sea Town can be."

"I don't want to talk about it," she said tartly.

"What? What's wrong, Sakura?" I became concerned.

"I can bike to my dorm and gather all my stuff. I'll move in with you." I was pleased to hear this.

"No. We can situate your bike to my car and I'll give you a lift the whole way." I offered.

"You sure?"

"Of course. Now, will you tell me what happened?"

Sakura hung her head low and frowned. She removed the glasses and I was shocked to see that she had a black eye.

"And you haven't called the police?" I was stunned. "Sakura, that man is insane! He just committed a crime in broad daylight and you're going to pretend that none of it happened? Also, that was completely racist of him to say to you. Highly inappropriate and unacceptable. That's not right. Your safety is paramount." I said this all angrily.

"I'm aware of that, Jenna. But I shouldn't have consulted him in the first place. It was partially my fault."

"It's not your fault at all. Don't let him get away with that. Stand up for yourself and fight for justice."

"I'm not like that, though."

"You should. If you don't, I'll do something." I said firmly, and I meant every word.

"No, Jenna. Don't. I don't want you involved. I'll do something."

"Like what?"

"You can go to class for me and take down notes from now on. I won't go to class." I felt as if I was just slapped in the face.

"Hey, I'm here to help you out, you know. But I won't go around doing everything for you. Besides, you can't just avoid it."

"I know," she admitted with a large frown.

"Don't worry, Sakura. That bastard isn't going to get away with this. I'll make sure of that." She stared at me curiously and questioned, "What are you going to do?" I told her I'd think about it. I assured her that he wasn't going to bother her or anyone ever again. She seemed confused by my proclamation, but I was determined and already formulated a plan to get sweet revenge.

CHAPTER ELEVEN

Jenna drove me to my little dorm, which was eight blocks away from the university. The campus to the University of Washeendom was so huge that all the dormitories had to be located a bit afar from the school. Jenna followed me to my room. It was small, unventilated, and untidy. When I entered the room, there were clothes strewed all over the place, and they all belonged to my roommate. I searched for my five large sports bags that contained all my clothes. Kayla's pink thong was on top of one of them. I carefully removed it and set it on the floor.

"I can understand why you agreed to move in with me." She laughed.

"Yeah." I grunted.

Jenna offered to carry the sports bags to her car as I held three large boxes that had my make-up, hygiene supplies, shoes, kitchen ware, electronic devices, and pictures of my family back home in Japan, Spain, and the Philippines. By the time we were finished, Jenna's trunk was full and so were the back seats.

"You got quite a bit of stuff." she commented.

"Yeah. Sorry about that."

"No worries mate. There's plenty of room at my place, you know. We can put all your stuff in the bedroom." She spoke in an Australian accent.

"Okedokie artichokie."

She giggled. I liked it a lot when she laughed. It gave me a nice tingly feeling.

We unloaded my things when we got back to her house. She was right; there was plenty of space in her bedroom for my stuff. As I unzipped my sports bags to organize my clothes, I heard Jenna's footsteps on the staircase. A loud, screeching sound was present, too. When she returned,

Jenna was accompanied with a large, wooden wardrobe that was identical to her own. I gawked at her.

"Well, what do you think? I had an extra wardrobe. You can have it." She pushed the empty wardrobe next to her own.

"Wow, Jenna. I love it! Thank you." I ran to her and gave her a hug. I could tell she wasn't expecting it.

"You're welcome, Sakura."

We held each other for a few seconds. It was nice because I could feel her heartbeat upon my bosoms. I sniffed her long, dark hair and it smelled like lavender. She loosened the embrace and said, "Let's get your things put away."

Jenna and I spent the evening sitting at her porch near the back door from the kitchen. We gazed at the sky, seeing very few stars. We each had a small bottle of ginger ale in our hands. I took a small sip from mine and said, "Wouldn't it be nice to see the sky filled with stars? Too bad there are too many lights in the city."

Jenna nodded and added, "I once got to see the stars here. All of them."

"How's that possible?"

"There was a black out along this block. I took a stroll outside as the repairmen came by to fix things. It was nice. The weather was decent, too."

"Oh." I said. "I think I was out of town when that happened. I was in Japan."

"Where in Japan?"

"Tokyo."

"You're a city dweller, huh."

"Yeah. I am. If I wasn't with my dad in Japan, I was in Manila with my mom, or visiting my grandmother in Alicante."

"I've been to Spain before, but only to Barcelona."

"It's pretty there." I commented. Jenna nodded.

"And hot. I got sunburned. That's why I like it here in Sea Town. The weather's moderate," she added. I nodded and asked, "Were you born here?"

"No. I was born in Perth, Australia. But I grew up there and in Sheffield, England. Mum's from Australia and Dad's from England."

"Oh. You lived near the coast of Western Australia, and in the northern part of England, huh."

"Yes. I did. I go back to visit family once every few years. I've lived here ever since my aunt died eight years ago."

An uncomfortable silence followed. It lasted for a few minutes. Jenna rested her head on my shoulder and took another sip of ginger ale.

"Do you want to go lay down on the hammock?" she suggested.

I could smell her warm breath when she spoke. Her hammock was yards away from us, attached between two large trees in her backyard. An orange shed was adjacent to it and a large, see-through sheet hung above the hammock. I assumed it was there to serve as a roof when it rained.

"Okay." I agreed.

Jenna stood up and ran to the hammock. She rocked back and forth in it. I walked over and sat on the edge.

"Come lay down with me," she said. She tugged on my arm. "It's comfy."

I slowly joined her, the side of our arms touching each other. Jenna took her last sip of ginger ale and placed the bottle on the grass. I was long finished with mine and placed it beside her bottle. She burped. I couldn't help but laugh. Jenna giggled and said, "Excuse me." I felt tired from the events of the day. My eyes felt heavy and my head began spinning. I didn't realize how tired I was until then. Yawning, I stretched my arms out and arched my back.

"Tired?" asked Jenna.

"Yeah. A little. It's been a long day."

"We can sleep here. If it rains, we'll remain dry."

"No…the bed's cozier…" I was drifting towards dreamland.

I could hear Jenna's giggling become fainter, fading into stupor. She whispered in my ear good night.

I woke up in the middle of the night and was shocked to see Jenna gone. I called out her name, but there was complete silence. A dark figure in a cloak loomed over the sheet that hung above the hammock. Its yellow eyes transfixed on me. I wanted to sink into the ground or completely vanish. The figure leaped off the sheet and stood beside me, its head next to the side of my face. The surreptitious being licked my ear and touched my thigh. I wanted to scream but couldn't. I winced and shut my eyes tightly, hoping that the individual would disappear. It spoke in a hoarse voice.

"What a lovely neck." it said. My lip quivered, and my body trembled. The figure felt cold as ice. "Don't worry. I won't hurt you. Stay with me, forever." It opened its mouth and showed a pair of long, white fangs. Its fangs sank into my neck. I screamed in pain.

CHAPTER TWELVE

My arm was wrapped around Sakura's soft belly and my head rested on her bosoms. I could feel her breathe steadily. Suddenly, she arched her back and screamed. She tossed her head left and right and kicked her legs in the air.

"Hey, Sakura. Wake up." I placed my hands on her shoulders and shook her. Her eyes flung wide open. Her expression was dazed.

"Are you okay?" I asked worriedly.

Her dark, beautiful brown eyes met with mine. She nodded and said she just had a nightmare. I was relieved. I asked her what she dreamt of.

"It's nothing, just a silly dream," she said. The subject was dropped.

I checked the time on my green wristwatch and it read five a.m. I told her it was still early. She snuggled against me like a frightened child curled into a ball. I soothed her nerves by singing a lullaby. My voice was soft-spoken and smooth. Within minutes, Sakura was quietly snoring. I held her close against my body; her figure warm and soft. I rubbed my cheek against hers and fell back to sleep, embracing her.

On Monday Sakura and I arrived at our psychology class and the instructor was absent. Everyone was huddled in small groups. I thought it was a bit amusing the way they separated themselves; it reminded me of high school. At the corner of the room were the preppy people; to the left were the gothic ones; to the right were the jocks; the nerdy-looking adults huddled in the front of the room; the punk group socialized at the center. Oddly enough, they were all discussing the same subject.

"Did you hear? The cops found Mr. Richard dead at his house at three o'clock Saturday morning. The killing was clean though. All they found his neck pierced and blood completely drained from their bodies. I bet they found 'em ghostly white." It was Robby who informed the entire class.

"Yeah, like he ain't white enough." someone joked. A few other people chuckled.

"I wonder who's responsible." Sally questioned. I couldn't stand her squeaky, mousy voice.

"Vampires?" Fred suggested.

"Blah! Those don't exist." Jack said stridently.

"Hasn't there been some evidence that they are around, like in documentaries?" asked Sally.

"Those findings were inconclusive, like video tapes of UFOs." Jack rebutted.

A heated debate followed whether vampires existed, and it seemed like half of the class was split between the sides. Sakura and I sat as spectators, listening to them argue and contradict one another. It was quite amusing. The dispute was on the verge of getting physical when Robby insulted Fred's family, accusing them of being stupid heretics.

"Take that back, Samson!" Fred shouted; his face flushed.

"Hell no, you Neanderthal." Robby retorted.

Fred was about to punch Robby when the door swung open and an elderly woman with short, fading, white hair walked in. Her voice was hoarse and shrill. She spoke to us condescendingly.

"I'm sorry everyone, but there will be no class today, or for the next month. It will take a long while before the district finds a decent enough teacher to take Mr. Richard's place. I'm sorry, but you all must leave. I hope you all respected your professor and remember the positive things he has done for every one of you in terms of educational improvement. Good day."

When she left, Robby muttered, "What educational improvement? None of us were enlightened at all. That old prick couldn't even teach if his life depended on it." Sally sauntered over to Robby and took his hand.

"Let's go home, Robby-poo." She cooed at him.

"Okay, Sally-poo." said Robby. He swung his head, tossing his bangs. They rubbed their noses together and kissed each other as they ambled off.

Forty-five minutes remained before my next course. Sakura and I spent that time chatting at an outdoor bench behind the school library. The sun glistened through the white clouds. The day was lovely and warm. Sakura brought along a bottle of water and retrieved it from her backpack. She started drinking from it. I took out a pack of cigarettes and offered one to her. She shook her head.

"No thanks. I don't smoke. I don't use substances, remember?" she said.

I nodded sympathetically. I told her it was a very good thing that she didn't smoke, and I advised her not to consider starting.

"Look who's talking." she said. "I should be the one nagging you not to continue such a habit."

"It's not a habit." I said curtly. "It's merely a stress reliever. Smoking helps me clear my mind out, you know. Plus, it calms me down, somewhat sedating me. Of course, you wouldn't know, would you?" I winked at her. Her face grew sad.

"Is anything wrong? What's stressing you?" She was concerned.

"Oh, nothing much. I just felt uneasy after that class. Mr. Richard's murder and all that. It's mind boggling."

"That's true. It's a mystery. But that's no excuse to go out and smoke. Ultimately, it kills you." Sakura said bitterly. "You should try other alternatives to relieve stress, like meditating or yoga. My grandfather died from emphysema. And I don't want you coming to that fate."

I slowly inhaled the cigarette, relishing its taste and gradually exhaled, sending smoky fumes to the air. I liked the smell that cigarettes gave off. Then I tossed it to the ground and smashed it with my foot.

"I'll try and quit, Sakura." I said solemnly.

"Okay," she said happily.

"Did you see Robby and Sally walk off together like a couple?" I asked. Sakura's eyes were sparkling as the sunlight shined on her pretty face.

"Yeah. I did." she said plainly. She added, "Robby isn't the kind of character that I want to be involved with. He seems too snobbish and arrogant for his own good."

"Sally has already slept with him a few times and bragged about how wonderful in bed he was. She told all her girlfriends about his large cock, too. She described it as 'King of all penises.'"

There was a long pause afterwards. I waited for her to say something. She finally asked, "How do you know all that?" I leaned forward into her face, our noses almost touching and said I was psychic. She giggled.

"Yeah, right." Sakura said doubtfully.

"Come on. Saying, 'I overheard Sally blabbering everything outside the Commons last week' is lame." I folded my arms and tilted my head to the side.

"Well, I guess I can call you the queen of all gossips, huh." she said. I smiled and nodded vigorously.

"Eavesdropping is my thing, you know. I should be a reporter or someone who writes the tabloids." I said mischievously.

"What a naughty lady." she teased. We both laughed.

"So, tell me, Sakura. Have you got any interest in the male anatomy?"

Sakura stared at me blankly and said, "I have no interest of discussing the male anatomy. I'll ignore your question."

"Come on. Don't be silly." I said.

"Why do you ask?"

"I'm curious."

"Tell me what you think first," she said, "Do you have any interest in the male anatomy?"

"Well, for myself, no. In a general sense I'm indifferent. I'm not interested in the male anatomy as a personal gain in any way. Hope that answers your question." I answered passively.

"I certain does. Very interesting."

"So, tell me, what is your stance?"

"Similar as yours. I'm indifferent and have no personal gain regarding it. It is what is."

"Okay. And the female anatomy? What are your thoughts on that?"

"I think the female anatomy is very lovely. I like it a lot. I guess you can say I am biased in my opinion. Yourself, Jenna?"

"Agreed," I big grin formed on my face. Sakura smiled back. Then I asked her, "What do you think about sex?"

"I have a positive outlook on sex. Between consenting adults. I'm also for safe sex. And sex as an act of love even though it isn't always like that for everyone. And a person being ready for it with the right person."

"Me, too. Looks like we have some things in common. Sex can be fun, too, you know. It's one of the things we as humans sought out to do; one of the great pleasures to life."

"I guess you aren't a virgin," she muttered.

I giggled, "Of course not. I've had some experience. I'm getting old, you know." She stared at me, disbelieved and asked how old I was.

"Twenty-nine." Her jaw dropped.

"I thought you were twenty-one!" She blushed.

"Why, thank you dear. But I am not that young anymore."

"You don't look like it." I shrugged.

"Being a virgin isn't a bad thing." I said.

"Who said I am a virgin?"

"I can tell. And that's fine. I admire people who have maintained their virginity through their late teens. I sure wasn't one of them."

"You're right, I am still a virgin. Honestly, I'm in no rush. How old were you when you first had sex?"

"Sweet seventeen."

"Wow, you are experienced."

"I guess so." I smiled at her as she grinned back.

CHAPTER THIRTEEN

I walked through the doorway of the wellness building and strolled outside. I just finished teaching martial arts and my back was sore from tumbling. All my pupils were gradually improving and whenever one performs a routine better than the last time, it makes me satisfied. That's the beauty of being a teacher in marital arts: knowing that you've helped someone improve his or her skills.

I walked towards the library to study chemistry. Along the way I spotted Robby at a bench, sitting alone. I walked faster, hoping he wouldn't see me. I didn't do a good job at it. Once he saw me, he waved and started lingering towards me, both his hands in his jeans. He wore a lime green sweater and black sneakers.

"Hi there." he greeted.

"Hello." I wanted to run away. He scrutinized my face.

"You're really flushed. Did you just work out?"

"Yeah. I teach martial arts here."

"Oh. That's cool. I know a little bit of karate."

Robby twirled his arms in a circular movement, fists clenched, and knees bent. He attempted to punch my shoulder, but I easily and swiftly blocked the attack with my hand. Firmly holding his wrist, I twisted his arm. Robby wined in pain.

"Okay, uncle! You win." He begged. I released my tight grip.

"Damn. You're one hardcore woman fighter. You need to teach me some of that stuff."

"Take the class sometime."

"How much?"

"The uniform is eighty dollars and classes are a hundred dollars bimonthly."

"Dang. That's pricey."

"I'm a good teacher though."

"How many students do you have?"

"There are three levels: beginning, intermediate, and advanced. Each class has twenty people. One session is an hour long. Each level meets at the wellness building daily. I teach part time."

"Wow, you must be filthy rich, huh."

"Not really. It pays the bills."

"I think I'll pass that offer, babe." He flung his bangs away from his eyes. I stared at him sternly.

"Don't call me babe." I said coldly.

"Gee. Okay lady. Don't start beating me up now." He laughed, but I didn't.

"Don't you have somewhere to go, or something to do?" I wanted him to leave.

"Nope. And why are you trying to get rid of me? I carried you to your friend's car when you were knocked out. Remember? You should be graveling in front of me and thanking me for my generosity."

"Well, thanks. But my friend was totally capable of carrying me."

"I was being a fine gentleman," he boasted, "And I think you owe me a free lesson."

"A fine gentleman as yourself wouldn't ask for anything in return." I snapped.

Robby winced and said, "Well, sorry. Looks like someone's having some major PMS issues today. You need to get that under control."

Neither of us said anything for a long moment. Robby tapped his foot on the ground, stretched his arms out and yawned. I finally spoke.

"I have to go. I'm a busy woman."

"Doing what?"

"Studying."

"See. That's what I like about you. Most of the chicks here are all about getting loaded or laid. Typical college girl for you. You on the other hand, are more ambitious and serious about studies. I like you a lot." I was speechless. Robby was the last person I expected to flirt with me.

"What about Sally?" I asked accusingly.

"That slut? Nah. She and I broke up. Besides, that Sally will date any guy who's willing to pull down his pants for her. She didn't like my performance. I guess I was too much for her."

"You're a nutcase." I said. He laughed.

"How about I take you out to dinner sometime? It'll give you a break from those textbooks."

"I'm not interested."

"Come on. I'm a good guy. I think you and I can really pull it off."

"No. I'm not interested." I repeated.

"Why not?"

"You're not my type."

"I can satisfy you, you know." He winked.

"You're sick. Stay away from me."

"Come on, Sakura. I just want to show you a good time. What's wrong with that?"

"Everything." I said bitterly. I turned and began running.

Robby grabbed my arm and pulled me close to him. His hands rested on my waist as he pinned me to a wall. My back faced the wall and his face was literally one inch away from mine. No one was in sight. He pressed himself against me. I could feel his crotch press firmly against mine. He ran his hand down my side until it reached my thigh.

"Don't be a bitch," he said maliciously. "I'm a man, and you deserve to experience what one can do for you. I'll pick you up here at seven. We'll go to dinner. Wear something revealing and loose tonight. Then we'll go to my place and I'll show you the best evening ever. I'll satisfy you like no man has ever done before. Gals don't call me the naughty, hardcore lover for nothing. You'll love it, babe. Trust me on this one. You'll burst in pleasure. Do I make myself clear?"

"Fuck you! I wouldn't have sexual intercourse with you if you were the last man alive!" I spat on his face.

CHAPTER FOURTEEN

I drove back to school that day and parked my vehicle across the street from the entrance. Sakura wasn't sitting on the steps where she usually would. I searched the perimeter, hoping to bump into her. After an hour of thorough investigation, Sakura was nowhere to be found. I was getting worried. I started calling out her name. I took out my cell phone from my pink purse and dialed her number. Her cell phone was off.

I saw Robby standing at the doorway of the wellness building. A white bandage was on his nose. Sally walked up to him and slapped him on the face. She sauntered away, ignoring him as he cursed at her. I hurried over to her.

"Sally, have you seen Sakura?" I asked. Sally looked at me. She was angry.

"No. And when you do, tell that bitch to fuck off my man." She belligerently continued walking.

"Wait, she was with Robby?" I clarified.

"Yeah. Go talk to him about it. I don't feel like talking."

I walked up to Robby and asked him where Sakura was.

"I don't know. I talked with her a half an hour ago. We shared a few laughs, had a few hugs. We made out here. It was a good time. She even wanted to try a threesome with Sally." He laughed, but I found his humor extremely crude. I didn't believe a word he said.

"Do you think I'm that stupid? What really happened?" He looked at me, dumbfounded by my direct accusation.

"I don't know what you mean, Jenna. But I honestly don't know where Sakura is. I'm sure she isn't too far away. Just to let you know, she and I are going on a date tonight. She'll be home late." A broad smile formed on his face. I glared at him and tugged on his green sweater.

"Listen. If you ever lay a finger on her, I guarantee you that you'll be seeing me right away and that will not be good for you at all."

"And what does that supposed to mean, missy? Are you threatening me?" He lifted his eyebrow. He moved his head closer to my face.

"No one messes with her and gets away with it." I warned.

"I'm not afraid of you, Jenna," he said stridently.

"You should be. I might not know martial arts, but I have my ways. I'm not afraid to use those tactics on some lowlife as yourself."

"What did you just call me?"

"You know what I said. Or are you deaf?" Robby's face turned red.

"Listen. You don't want to make me mad. You hear me?" he said.

"Why don't you follow your own advice? You don't want to mess with me. Crazy things have been going around here, like Mr. Richard's murder. It would be a pity if you have the same fate."

"What the hell does that mean?"

"Just telling you to be careful." I lowered my face and curled my forehead, demonstrating a malicious expression.

"You're as queer as Sakura," he said. He turned around and strutted off.

I felt so frustrated when I drove home after not finding Sakura on campus. Anxiety took over me. My mind paced quickly. Numerous thoughts of what happened to Sakura twirled in my mind. Appointment? No. She would have informed me in advance. Yearned for time to be away from me? No. She enjoyed my company. Left the country? No. She didn't have a good reason to do so. One suggestion led to another until my mind hurt and I got a headache. I dialed her cell phone number again, hoping that she had it on. There was only her voicemail.

"Hello. You've reached Sakura Hatsukawa. I'm busy now but leave your number and message after the beep, and I'll get back to you as soon as possible." The voicemail informed. I waited for the beep.

"Hey, Sakura. It's me. I came by to pick you up, but you weren't there. Let me know where you are, okay? You know my number, so give me a call. Ta ta." I hung up and continued driving.

I noticed Sakura's bike at the driveway near the garage of the house. Filled with hope, I ran into the house and called her name multiple times. I searched throughout the for fifteen minutes and was depressed to find her not there.

"Where are you, Sakura?" I thought miserably.

CHAPTER FIFTEEN

Robby slapped me hard. My cheek stung.

"Aren't you a feisty one? Don't be an impish. You're disappointing me, babe," he whispered.

I struggled, trying to break free from the uncanny, discomfort position, but he didn't budge. Situating his palms on the brick wall, he leaned on me hard. His crotch more firmly placed against mine to add more pressure. I tried to push him off, but his feet were firmly glued to the ground.

"You feel me, baby?" He chuckled and continued harassing me. I was desperate. I needed to act fast. I opened my mouth to scream, but Robby covered my mouth with his large, sweaty hand.

"Don't you dare scream. Or you'll end up like old Mr. Richard." His blue eyes glowered, "That bastard deserved what was coming."

I was terrified and felt helpless and powerless. He took his hand off my mouth.

"You murdered Mr. Richard!" I blurted. He covered my mouth again. "Robby, please stop," I pleaded while muffled.

"Shut up. That's a goddamn lie, and you know it. You know nothing. I didn't kill that bastard, you hear me? I've been fantasizing about this day ever since I carried you to Jenna's car. I see that you two have been bonding lately. That won't last if I'm around, baby." he whispered in my ear, smirking.

"You're an asshole." I said, muffled by his hand. He understood my slur and chuckled again. It bothered me when he did that. I didn't want to give him any satisfaction.

Just then, I had an idea. I absolutely didn't want to do it, but I knew I had to try. I quickly slid my hand down to his crotch and squeezed as hard as I could, twisting it. Robby yelped painfully and flinched. I punched his face, giving him a bloody nose and kicked him hard in the groin. He fell to the ground, his hands covering his crotch, groaning. I sprinted away from the school, never looking back. Tears streamed down my cheeks. I never felt so violated in such an aggressive manner. Robby managed to tear my shirt so that my bra was exposed. I was in shock and so much in tears.

I ran to the parking lot where my bike was parked between two other bicycles. I biked to school during the weekend and left it there for a few days when I was staying at Jenna's. I leaped on it and started pedaling towards Jenna's house. My breathing was heavy, and my knees were sore. Several times I adjusted my shirt to cover my bra.

"I'm such an idiot!" I thought. I should've run when Robby approached me. Tears rolled down my face. My feelings were hurt. I felt stupid and silly. *"Why can't I be strong like Jenna? This totally sucks."*

I finally reached Jenna's house. I was able to get inside because she made a duplicate key for me the other day. I entered the bedroom and searched my wardrobe for clean clothes. Quickly changing my shirt, I slipped on a baby blue top. I hid my ripped shirt in one of the drawers.

I opened my backpack and pulled out my planner. I looked at it, skimming at tasks that had to be done for the day. Under Monday, it read: Doctor's appointment. 6 p.m. Evernette. I looked at my silver watch and it was ten minutes until three. Evernette was very far, so I decided to get there by bus. I left the house, locking the door after I grabbed something to eat. With a cinnamon roll in my mouth, I slid my wallet in my back pocket and walked a few blocks to catch the bus.

CHAPTER SIXTEEN

I sat alone on the porch with a cigarette in my mouth and slowly smoked it until it was as tiny as an eraser tip of a pencil. I played the radio loudly from the kitchen and listened to the traffic jam update along interstate ninety-one. There was a shooting at a Safepath grocery store in Evernette. Two armed men were arrested and pleaded innocent to the numerous charges they faced. A news report notified that a young girl drowned at Bluelake after being strangled to death. The mother of the girl was now a primary suspect. I listened aimlessly, almost dosing to sleep. After a few intermissions and advertisements there was breaking news.

"Just in, folks." The news woman began, "A college student by the name of Robby Samson, roughly twenty-two-years-old was found dead in his dormitory located at the University of Washeendom around seven o'clock this evening. He was naked and strapped to his bedpost. The man's neck was pierced, and no trace of blood was detected anywhere. The crime was like that of Mr. Richard's case that occurred over the weekend. It was however, different because Robby had his genitals stuffed in his mouth. On his bed stand were packages of cocaine and methamphetamine, in addition to needles with herion."

"What we have here are unacceptable atrocities. We, the police, will not tolerate another incident like this to happen in our homely neighborhoods. We are doing all we can to hunt down this serial killer," said a policeman.

"Lieutenant Charles, there are rumors circulating, all claiming the killer is immortal. More specifically, a vampire that's roaming through the streets," stated the news woman.

"The killer has an eerie taste for blood, but I assure you, we are facing with a human being here. The city of Sea Town will get rid of this madman as soon as possible. Meanwhile, the school district has closed the University for security purposes. The school won't reopen until further notice."

I listened keenly, carefully absorbing every word.

"That's all the news we've obtained on this story. Join us later tonight at eleven o' clock for more information and local news. Thank you for listening to Kilo seven eyewitness news, your most reliable news source in Sea Town." The brief theme song followed.

I turned off the radio and helped myself to a glass of water. It was nine o'clock and Sakura hadn't come home or returned my call. I called again but didn't leave a message. Feeling exhausted, I wanted to go to bed early. I got ready after an hour and lay awake.

I gazed at the ceiling. My body laid motionless and my mind stressed out. I couldn't sleep not knowing how Sakura was doing. I wanted to hear from her more than anything. Suddenly, I heard soft footsteps in the hallway. The door slowly opened, and Sakura walked inside, tiptoeing to her wardrobe and rummaged for clean clothes to wear. I pretended I was asleep, my eyelids half-opened as I watched her undress. She put on her purple pajamas, tossed her dirty clothes in the laundry hamper next to the bathroom, and quietly crawled into bed.

CHAPTER SEVENTEEN

After my appointment with Dr. Miller, I stopped by Safepath, a local grocery store. I walked along the deli section and bought a small tray of sushi, my favorite food. As I approached the doorway, two men dressed in black, wearing Frankenstein masks entered. They each pulled out a gun and pointed it aimlessly at the crowd.

"Everyone stop!" shouted one of the bandits.

The other shot a bullet through the ceiling. People screamed and scrambled to get to the exit. The same man fired another shot, and everyone fell silent. I ducked down to the ground, both my hands covering the back of my head.

One of the men ran to the cashiers and demanded that they hand over all their money. The other man stood pointing the gun to as many people as he could, trying to look threatening. All the employees cooperated and handed the burglar all the cash, stuffing it all in a large sack. The burglar slowly walked backwards towards his partner, pointing his gun at the crowd. Someone close by quickly took out his cell phone and dialed 911. One of the men shot him dead. Blood splattered on the floor. Women and children screeched. The crooks ran off, hurrying to their vehicle.

Filled with anger, impulse, and stupidity, I sprinted after them. I took one of the men by surprise and snatched his gun. I shot his foot and he fell to the ground, groaning. The other fired at me, but I dodged the hit and shot his foot, too. He dropped his gun, along with the sack of money. I quickly grabbed the other gun and emptied both weapons of their bullets. I took the sack and hurried back into the store where people gathered around the shot man, trying to help him. One of the crooks managed to run in massive pain after me and jumped on my back. I fell to the ground. His entire weight was on my back as he pulled my hair.

"You bitch! You shot my fucking foot!" he said furiously.

I relied on my side vision to predict his movements. Before he could punch me, I turned around and swiftly wrapped my legs around his throat in a locking position. He tried to pull my legs off but couldn't. Using the strength of my legs and flexibility, I pushed him backwards, forcing him to land on his back. I quickly stood up, faced him, and pressed my foot against his throat. Leaning forward, I whispered bitterly in his ear, "You've messed with the wrong lady." I punched him hard in the face. He fell unconscious. His partner was already knocked out. The police arrived within minutes. By then I was long gone after returning the money to the store. I walked to the bus stop, sat at a bench, and waited.

A tall, slim woman with short, blonde hair approached the bus stop. She sat next to me. She wore a brown fur coat, wore lots of make-up, and stank with perfume. She dressed quite revealingly. She looked at me with her hazel eyes and started talking.

"That was amazing what you did back there." she commented.

"Thanks." I said quietly. I wasn't in the mood for talking to anyone.

"What's your name? I'm Cindy. Cindy Hendricks. I own a hospital in Downtown."

"I'm Sakura. Sakura Hatsukawa." I avoided as much eye contact as I could.

"How did you learn to fight?"

"My father taught me. He was a martial arts teacher."

"That's amazing. Wish I could fight like that."

"It takes years of practice."

"I bet. Are you really waiting for the bus? It's late. It's nearly nine. Where do you live?"

"Near the University of Washeendom."

"Good Lord! That's several miles from here. I'll give you a ride home."

"No thank you. I can take the bus."

"You're kidding. Come on. If we go by car, it'll take only a half an hour. It's about three times as long if you take the bus. Be reasonable." I was tired and the thought of not having to wait for buses was favorable. I agreed.

The ride with Cindy was longer than I anticipated. There was much traffic and it was raining hard. The radio was on. We listened to the Kilo station.

"Just in, folks." The news woman began, "A college student by the name of Robby Samson, roughly twenty-two-years-old was found dead in his dormitory located at the University of Washeendom…" I turned up the volume. "…The killer has an eerie taste for blood, but I assure you, we are facing with a human being here. The city of Sea Town will get rid of this madman as soon as possible. Meanwhile, the school district has closed the University for security purposes. The school won't reopen until further notice…"

"Wow," said Cindy. "A lot of crazy things have been happening recently."

"Yeah." I said. I was shocked by the news. School was completely closed until further notice.

"Looks like you aren't going to school for a while." she emphasized.

"I guess so."

"How do you feel about that?"

"Utterly bewildered and unexpected."

She laughed and said, "You're a funny one. What's your major?"

"Psychology with a future in medicine as a medical doctor."

"Oh. That's interesting."

"Yeah."

"Well, good luck with that."

"Thanks."

"You're welcome."

We said nothing the rest of the way. Cindy dropped me off a block away from the house because I told her that I lived right there. I thanked her for the ride and she drove away noisily. I hurried to the house. I looked at my watch and it was nearly eleven-thirty.

CHAPTER EIGHTEEN

I turned over on my side. I faced Sakura's back and I tapped her shoulder. She didn't move, so I blew into her ear. She turned over to lie on her back and turned her head towards me.

"Hi," she said. "I thought you were asleep."

"No. I've been up thinking and worrying about you. Where did you go? Did you get my call?" I could tell she knew I was disappointed.

"I'm sorry. I should have told you in advance. I had an appointment with the doctor in Evernette and I took the bus."

"I thought you were with Robby." I said hurtfully.

"No way. I would never do that. I hate that guy. I was however, at the Safepath where the shooting took place. Did you hear about it?"

I looked at her, disbelieved. She stared at me seriously.

"Yes. I heard it on the radio. You were really there?"

"Yup. And I stopped the thieves. They were armed, too."

"Sakura, that's dangerous! What if something happened to you?"

"But nothing did. Is that what matters? Besides, I couldn't let those loons get away with what they were doing."

"I wish you thought that way towards Mr. Richard." I said.

"This is different. This was a life and death situation and many more people were involved. Innocent people."

"Whatever." I still wasn't happy that she didn't call.

"What made you think I was with Robby?" she asked.

"He told me you had a date with him tonight when I went around looking for you this afternoon. I wasn't sure if he was telling the truth."

"Well, he did hit on me. But I told him I wouldn't go out with him."

"And he had a broken nose. Do you know what happened?" She didn't answer. Instead, she rolled on her side away from me and remained quiet. I grew worried.

"What's wrong?" I asked.

"Nothing," she grunted.

"I can tell if something's wrong, Sakura. You get quiet suddenly."

"I don't want to talk about it, Jenna." I put my arm around her, covering her belly.

"I'm here to listen," I whispered in her ear.

"I know." she said tearfully. She began to weep. I felt dreadful.

"You got to tell me what's bothering you, or else I can't help. What's the matter? Sakura?"

She didn't say a word. She cried. She turned over and buried her head in my bosoms and embraced me tightly. I let her cry in my arms and said nothing. After a few minutes, she finally stopped crying. I wiped her tears.

"Look what you've done to your face, silly." I teased. She frowned.

"I'm sorry. I'm such a baby. I probably annoy you."

"No. It's okay. You can tell me whatever you like. Besides, it's okay to have an emotional breakdown occasionally. I'm sure it's for a good reason. So, are you ready to share with me what happened today? I'm guessing it has to do with Robby, huh."

"Uh huh." She nodded and told me the whole story.

CHAPTER NINETEEN

Jenna listened attentively, not blinking once. When I was done, her lips were pursed, and her face was somber. Nervously, I waited for her feedback.

"Well, at least you beat him up. But you should have ran for help instead of leaving him with minor marks. He's such a sexist, misogynistic, entitled pig filled with narcissism."

"I figured I tortured him enough."

"Not good enough. His punishment does not suit his actions at all. He should have gone to jail for what he did."

"That doesn't matter now. He's dead."

"Yes. It's a pity how he died. He had it coming though."

I felt suspicious. "What do you mean by 'he had it coming?'" I questioned.

"Karma." she said.

"Sure." I said sarcastically.

"Don't tell me you don't believe in karma." She seemed shocked.

"I don't. And someone is out there committing these scary murders and it's creeping me out."

"Don't worry. You're safe here with me," she said reassuringly.

"Why do you say that?" I speculated.

"Because we both kick ass."

I laughed. Jenna smiled. We remained in each other's arms, cuddled in the large bed. No longer was I resting at the edge of the bed and Jenna at the other end. We met as one in the center and it was nice. Her eyes were closed, but I could tell she was still awake.

"Jenna," I whispered.

"Yes." she answered.

"Thank you. Thanks for everything." I kissed her cheek.

She held me tightly, our warm bodies touching. I could feel her slow heartbeat as mine pounded fast. At that moment, I was blushing stupidly. Jenna opened her eyes and saw me. She stroked my cheek.

CHAPTER TWENTY

"You're so cute when you blush." I told Sakura, removing my hand from her face.

"I can't help it. You make me feel…" she didn't complete her sentence.

"How do I make you feel, Sakura?" I gazed into her deep, dark brown eyes, mesmerized.

"Um. I don't know."

"Of course, you know silly." I giggled.

"I mean, it's hard to describe."

"There's more than one way of communicating. One is through speech, which can't describe everything. There just aren't enough words to accurately describe everything we feel or what we experience. But body language is the universal language." I pressed my nose against hers, feeling her breath gently blow on my face.

"You're right." she said.

"So, if you can't tell me what you're feeling, why don't you show me?"

She gazed at me, silent.

CHAPTER TWENTY-ONE

"I'm not ready for such a big step, Jenna." I finally said. I knew that she was in the mood and I was too, but I was too nervous.

"I understand. I was uncertain my first time. I can wait. Let's take it slow."

"Have you been with a girl?" I asked.

"Several times." I was surprised.

"Guys?"

"No. I prefer women."

"Oh." I said.

"I hope that doesn't offend you."

"No, it doesn't. I prefer women, too. I just never dated before."

"Why not?" Jenna asked curiously.

"I feel like I don't have what it takes to be a good partner."

"Don't say that. You'll make a great partner, Sakura." She winked. I blushed again.

"Why? What makes you so sure?"

"You should know that. You're sweet, loving, and sexy."

"Thanks. When I first saw you, I thought you were magnificently gorgeous."

"I thought you were quite dashing, darling." she said. I giggled.

"Have you ever kissed a girl on the lips?" she asked.

"No. But I always dreamed of it."

"Would you like to experience it now? With me?" Jenna face slowly moved towards my face.

My mind raced. I wanted to say, "Yes! I do! Let's do it!" but I couldn't speak. Before I knew it, my lips were on Jenna's. Her lips were warm, soft, and luscious. Kissing her felt so good. I was in paradise. I opened my mouth and her tongue entered, twirling inside. The kiss was longer than I expected. It was only for a few minutes, but I wanted it to last forever. Jenna broke the kiss and looked at my face.

"What do you think?" she asked.

"Can I have seconds? Please?" I asked. She giggled.

"You're silly. Of course," she said, and we kissed again.

CHAPTER TWENTY-TWO

The next morning was a typical rainy day in Sea Town. I had an itch to go outside and prance in the weather. Instead, I lay in bed beside Sakura who was still sleeping. She snored quietly, her head upon my bosoms. My hand rested on her waist. I closed my eyes, smiling when the phone suddenly rang. Sakura stirred and rolled over on her side so that her back was facing me. I climbed out of bed and walked towards the windowsill. The phone was located on a table next the windowsill. I answered it.

"Hello?"

"Jenna." It was mum.

"Hi mum. How are you?"

"I'm fine sweetheart. How's Sea Town?"

"Rainy."

"Well, that's pretty typical isn't it? Is everything okay? Did you get my check?" "Yes, mum. I just got it yesterday." Mum sends a thousand dollars every month just in case I needed it.

"Good."

"Thank you."

"Oh, did you hear? I'm getting married next week." My jaw dropped.

"To whom?"

"Gregory. Who else?" Gregory was an architect who's been dating her for three years. I met him once when I flew back home to visit Mum. He always dressed as a businessman, wearing a dark suit and matching tie. Australian bred, Gregory had broad shoulders, slick, black hair, and green eyes.

"Well, I'm happy for you, Mum. Gregory's a very lucky man."

"Thank you, Jenna. It would be nice if you could show up to the reception. Your father is coming, too."

"Aww, mum. I wouldn't miss it for the world."

"So, how's school?"

"It's fine." I didn't inform her about the killings or shut down.

"Are you getting good grades? Are the people there nice? Let me know if there's anything wrong. I don't want anyone pushing my baby around." She laughed.

"No, mum. Everything's fine. My grades are coming along well, and I made a new friend."

"Who is it? Is it a gentleman?"

"No mum. A young lady. Her name is Sakura. She's very nice."

"Well, that's good. I'm sure prince charming will come along very soon. I have such a beautiful, irresistible daughter. You got it from me, you know. I didn't meet your father until I was your age and I didn't marry him until ten years later."

"But you had me less than a year after you met him." I reminded her.

"Well, we all make spontaneous decisions, dear. But believe me, your birth was the best thing that ever happened to your father and me. I wouldn't trade it for anything in the world. You'll understand what I mean when you have children, Jenna. I love you so much and your father and I are extremely proud of you."

"Thanks, mum."

"See, I told you you'd find someone nice to bond with. Does she go to the same school?"

"Yes. We have the same class first period."

"How splendid!" she said enthusiastically.

"Indeed." I agreed.

"I bet you two are like sisters," she said.

"We're already very close."

"That's wonderful, dear."

"Thanks, mum."

CHAPTER TWENTY-THREE

Jenna placed the receiver back to its base and crawled back into bed. She lied on her back and folded her hands on her abdomen. I rolled over, facing her, and held one of her hands. Our fingers intertwined. She pulled herself closer to me until our bodies pressed one another.

"How's your mother?" I asked.

"She's fine. Did you hear everything?"

"Everything that you said."

"Well, she's having a wedding next week. Do you want to come?"

"Isn't that a family thing? I don't want to intrude."

"Family and friends are invited."

"Okay. We would have to go to Australia, huh."

"Yes. Don't worry about the cost, though. Mum is rich. She's the CEO of an international car company, and she's president of the entire industry that manufactures cricket equipment. She'll pay for both of us."

"Wow, Jenna. You really do come from a wealthy family. My family's working class. Mom's a painter and a nurse, and Dad's a musician and martial arts teacher. What does your father do?"

"Daddy's a neurosurgeon. He has a good reputation in England."

"I bet. That's amazing."

"So are you, Sakura."

Blushing, I said, "Thanks."

Saturday afternoon we drove to Upgate Mall, bickering along the way.

"No. That's not right. It's most likely male. It had to be someone strong enough to overpower him. How else could the victim have been pinned and strapped to the bed like that?" I asked. We were talking about the killer's profile, using Robby's death as a scenario.

"I disagree. I bet Robby was drugged first and returned to his dorm intoxicated. Lust elicited him to get to bed undressed. It had to be female in this case. There were no signs of struggle. Every move made was deliberate."

"What about Mr. Richard? He was found in his basement with bruises on his body."

"I bet the killer pushed him down the stairs. The older you get, the less balance you have."

"What makes you so sure it's a woman?" I interrogated.

"What makes you certain that it isn't?"

"You answer my question first. I already explained why the killer is probably male."

"Well, I've made my points, too. No need to repeat them."

"My argument's better." I wined.

"Ha! Mine isn't a theory like yours. Where's your evidence?"

"The proof is right there in your face! I don't have you tell you. Figure it out for yourself." I said quickly.

I turned my head and faced the window, watching other cars passed by. We didn't say a word for a few minutes. Jenna finally spoke.

"Frankly, I think the killer's an *it*."

"An *it*?"

"Yes. An immortal. Probably a vampire." I laughed.

"There's no such thing. That's a bunch of garbage."

"It's not rubbish. I think it might be."

"Why?" I asked.

"My intuition tells me. And I believe it."

"That's ridiculous. Vampires don't exist, just like ghosts, goblins, trolls, monsters, werewolves, and so forth. Those creatures were created for entertainment purposes."

"Well, as a citizen of this country, I have my right to an opinion." she said proudly.

"Yup." I nodded.

CHAPTER TWENTY-FOUR

The trip to Upgate Mall was an experience that was everything but pleasant. Sakura fled to the restroom after we went shopping. She bought four large bags filled with skirts, sandals, tank tops, blouses, jeans, and makeup. I carried a small bag of bras and panties. I stood near the restrooms, leaning against the wall in the empty hallway with several shopping bags surrounding my feet. The door to the women's lavatory swung opened. I thought it was Sakura, but it was Sally.

Sally saw me, obviously shocked by my presence. I reluctantly waved at her. She didn't look happy at all to see me. In fact, she appeared infuriated. My gut told me that this coincidence was going to turn sour. She stomped over to me. Her fists were clenched at her waist. My arms were folded, and I stood motionless, but causally. When she was within earshot, I asked, "Hello. How can I help you?" The query was asked in a sincere manner that an attendant would pose. Sally ignored my friendliness and glowered at me. She was starting to scare me a little bit.

"I know your secret. Don't pretend to act innocent. I can see through you, you moron," she said bitterly.

"Excuse me?" I said. I was speechless.

"Don't be stupid, you idiot. You murdered Robby, didn't you? You sick bitch!" She pushed me hard.

"Whoa. I did not do that." I felt victimized.

"Yes, you did. Admit it!" She screamed at my face. A crowd of people stopped and watched us. I felt embarrassed. I wanted to seal her mouth with duct tape.

"Sally calm down. You're disturbing others. You'll scare the little children away. It's too early for Halloween, you know." I whispered.

"Shut up! You think this is a fucking joke? You can't tell me what to do." Then she slapped me. I glared at her, exposing my teeth, grinding them.

"That was uncalled for." I said angrily.

"I saw you threatening Robby that day. He already had a broken nose. Give him some slack! That bitch of yours messed him up." I grabbed her turtleneck and zoomed my head at her small face.

"Don't you dare call her that. Do you understand? That asshole came onto her, you know. He deserved that broken nose." I said maliciously. I let go of her sweater.

Sally stood in front of me, stiff and unmoving. Her face was red and stern. Her body started to tremble violently for a brief few seconds. She seemed like she was going to explode any second. Instead, she stomped her foot, turned around and started walking off. Suddenly, she swiftly turned around, charged up to me, and punched me in the stomach. The hit was hard and painful. I winced and fell to my knees. Sakura stepped out from the bathroom. Her mouth fell when she saw us.

"Jenna!" Sakura hurried to my side and knelt beside me. "Are you okay?" Sally looked at us, her fists tightly curled. "What did you do?" Sakura asked Sally angrily.

"That fucking bitch deserved it. She messed with my Robby-poo."

"That asshole doesn't even like you, Sally." Sakura retorted.

"You slept with him, too huh. Did he satisfy you, Sakura? Fuck you!" she said accusingly.

"Sally, he's dead now. Forget about Robby and move on with your life. I'm sure you have better things to do than to pick a fight with us," said Sakura. I nodded in agreement. My belly was sore.

"But it's Jenna's fault that he's dead. She's responsible. That bitch of yours doesn't deserve to see another light of day."

Sakura slowly stood up, spread her legs shoulder width apart, bended her knees, and raised her clenched fists to her face.

"Sally, I'm warning you. I'm a martial arts expert and you don't want to mess with me. Why don't you just leave before things get dirty?"

Sally took a step forward and got into position the same way as Sakura.

"I'm a black belt in taekwondo. I've won loads of tournaments and got a room full of trophies."

"I didn't request for a lame inventory. I bet all your opponents were amateurs." Sakura said tartly.

"Shut up! You know nothing. You're a naïve disgrace for an Asian."

"What could you possibly know about Asians?"

"Everything. I grew up around them, smart-ass."

"You seem to lack the knowledge."

"You're just jealous."

"Why would I ever be jealous of you?"

"Because I got laid from the King of all cocks himself." She laughed.

"What a waste of time."

"Oh yeah? I bet you're still a virgin."

"You talk too much."

"Okay. Let's fight. I'll kick your ass. Then you'll be sorry and act more carefully when it comes to messing with me."

"I warned you Sally, but you leave me with no other choice. This just got personal."

I stared at Sakura and I've never seen her so serious until that very moment. It sent shivers up my spine.

"Let's take this outside." Sally declared.

"Bring it on." Sakura sneered.

"Sakura. Don't…" I beseeched. I dread that this would happen. She glanced down at me and whispered: "Don't worry. This will be a quickie." Then she winked, apparently confident.

The three of was walked outside to the parking lot, along with a huge crowd that witnessed our dispute. Several people circled around Sakura and Sally, patiently waiting for the fight to begin. I stood a few feet away from them. My mind was spinning. A part of me didn't want Sakura to fight because I didn't want to her to get hurt, but another part wanted to see Sally marred. The women took a few minutes to stretch and warm up.

"Look at them. This match looks official," said an old, bold fellow behind me.

"I bet that white chick is going to win," whispered a scruffy man next to the bold fellow.

"Naw. I'm betting on the Asian chick. She's hella hot," said a teenage boy.

The three of them started betting money on the winner. Not before long, the entire crowd was involved in the gambling. I ignored them and unwearyingly waited for the fight to be over.

Sakura was true to her word. The fight was quick, but it turned deadly. Sally took the offense by throwing punches at Sakura, but Sakura was able to block each one. Sakura jumped and tried to do an air kick, but Sally ducked. Then she immediately stood up and kicked Sakura. I held my breath as Sally got on top of her adversary and began choking her.

Struggling for air, Sakura quickly launched an arm at her challenger's face and poked her eyes. Sally cringed, stood up, and walked backwards. She covered her hands with her face. Sakura stood up and waited for her opponent's next maneuver.

Removing her hands from her face, Sally reached into her pocket and pulled out a pistol. Everyone who was cheering for his or her winner went silent. Sally fired, but Sakura dodged the bullet. Instead, it hit a little girl in the crowd. Her mother squealed, hurrying to her wounded daughter. Sally didn't stop. She pointed the gun at Sakura and shot multiple times. However, Sakura rolled on the ground and avoided every hit.

"Why won't you die, you bitch?" screamed Sally.

Two police cars came driving to the parking lot. The crowd quickly dispersed. The mother wept, cradling her bleeding child. A police officer pointed his gun at Sally as another spoke loudly.

"Put down the gun and no one will get hurt," warned the officer.

Sally tossed the weapon in the air and started running away. I sprinted after her and landed on her back, locking her arms behind her rear. One of the policemen hurried over and thanked me for helping. He handcuffed Sally and escorted her to the police car. Sally hollered at Sakura and I as she struggled to escape.

"It's not over yet! I will avenge Robby's death and hunt the two of you down! I'll make you pay, you fucking—" One of the policemen sealed her mouth, muffling the rest of what she had to say. In less than a minute, the police cars drove away. The sirens droned from the distance. An ambulance came and took the little girl and her mother to a hospital.

I felt so sorry for the little girl that before help arrived, I handed the mother a few thousand dollars to pay for the hospital fee or any possible operations that were needed for her daughter's recovery.

"God bless your heart," said the mother. There were tears in her eyes. Then she hugged me.

CHAPTER TWENTY-FIVE

"No. I'm fine. Really." Jenna insisted.

"Lie down." I told her. I pulled up her shirt and found a purple spot on her belly. I gently pressed it and asked if it hurt. She said it didn't, but the mark felt tender and looked painful.

"Don't worry about it, Sakura. I'll be okay."

"I'm getting you an ice pack just in case. Stay here."

"Wait." she said, grabbing my wrist. She pulled me towards her and kissed me.

"What was that for?" I asked, smiling.

"For standing up for me today, promising that the fight would be short, and not badly injuring yourself." she explained.

"Wow. I should get into fights for you more often." I joked. She hit my arm playfully.

"You silly." she said.

I stuck my tongue out at her and walked to the freezer in the kitchen. I came back with the ice pack and placed it on her bruise.

CHAPTER TWENTY-SIX

Sunday morning was spent cleaning the house. Sakura and I split the tasks. She swept the floors and cleaned the kitchen as I tidied up the bedroom, living room, dining room, and cleaned both bathrooms. She offered to do the laundry when she was done. I agreed and showed her the washer and dryer in the basement. Sakura turned on the radio in the living room loudly and we listened to the news as we worked.

"Thank you for joining us on Queen Three news, your station for news coverage. Police report a fighting last night at the south parking lot of Upgate Mall. A seven-year-old girl was shot. The girl's name was Lisa Truman. She's now in critical condition at a hospital in Downtown. The conflict started between two women, whom witnesses claimed attend University of Washeendom. One of the women, Sally Field, was arrested for shooting Lisa and assaulting the other woman as witnesses declared she began the conflict. Field is now in custody by the Queen County jail in Downtown where she pleads innocent of all charges..." I turned off the radio because I didn't want to hear the rest of it.

I took Sakura out to lunch when we finished cleaning. We ate at a Subpath restaurant in Dollard. I had a salad and she ordered a turkey sandwich.

"What made you want to be vegetarian?" she asked.

"For ethical reasons. I don't eat animals. I believe all animals deserve a full life. I believe their life is as valuable as any human being. Also, being vegetarian has been great for my health. I don't find meat all that appetizing either." I poked a cherry tomato with my fork and put it in my mouth.

"I tried to be vegetarian before, but I couldn't do it. It's too hard. Each time I tried I relapsed on seafood. I might be able to be pescatarian, but that would be hard for me, too." She took another bite of her sandwich.

"I understand. It's not an easy transition to make for everyone. In my case, it was a smooth transition as meat never really was an interest. As a vegetarian for many years, I don't fully understand how you could feed off the flesh, even if it's cooked of another creature without vomiting afterwards." I said.

"I admire your way of being vegetarian and respect that. I'm still an omnivore and will probably be one for a lifetime."

"That's okay. I'll be the vegetarian and you be the omnivore." I nodded and silently consumed what was left of my salad. I offered her a few of my croutons.

"Really? That's the best part in a Caesar salad."

"I know, but I'm getting full."

"Okay. If you insist." she said.

"I do."

CHAPTER TWENTY-SEVEN

"Hey, it's her. It's that chick that kicked that other chick's butt at the mall a few nights ago." Someone who sat across from our table whispered. He was a large man with a long, black, bushy beard and small spectacles. A teenage boy with long red hair accompanied him. He looked at me with his hazel eyes, awed. They both walked to our table and introduced themselves.

"I'm Jeff Romano and this is my friend Nick Truman," said the bearded man.

"Hi." said Nick. "Can I have your autograph?" He took out a pen and sheet of paper from his pocket.

"We're your biggest fans," added Jeff. I thanked them and wrote my signature.

"Hey." Nick turned to Jenna. "Aren't you that lady that got hit in the stomach by that other woman? Man, that was crazy. Can I get your autograph, too?"

"Sure, mate. Name's Jenna. Don't wear it out." Jenna took the pen, signed her name on it and winked at Nick. Nick blushed.

"Teach us some of that fighting stuff." Jeff said to me.

"I teach classes at the University, but the college closed down for investigations. So, when it opens again, you can register. Here's my card." I handed him my business card. "Call me if you're interested."

"Thanks." said Jeff. He and Nick strolled off. Jenna laughed.

"Did you see that?" she asked. She spoke in an Australian accent. "They actually asked for our autographs. It's like we're celebs. How bloody cool is that?" I grinned and nodded.

As we were driving home, I turned the radio on. One of my favorite songs was playing. I wasn't sure of the actual title of it. Nonetheless, I started to sing when it began. Jenna knew of the song and sang along. We sang and danced in our seats until we reached home.

When we got home, we were surprised to see a police vehicle parked across the street. A policewoman stood outside waiting at the front yard. We parked the car in the garage. Jenna and I got out and met with the woman.

"Hello, officer." Jenna greeted her in her friendly way.

"Hi." I said.

"Hello ladies. Are any of you Jenna Watson?" Jenna nodded.

"Good. I'm also looking for Sakura Hatsukawa." I raised my hand.

"Perfect. Will you two ladies come with me?"

"Sure," we said. We followed the woman to the car and she drove us to the police station.

CHAPTER TWENTY-EIGHT

When we reached the station, Sakura and I got separated. I followed the policewoman to a room as another female officer escorted Sakura to a different room. The room was white and bare, only containing a small wooden table and a few chairs. The woman interrogated me for some time. She had a tape recorder with her and a notepad and pen.

"I will be interviewing you for the next several minutes, Jenna. Will you cooperate and answer all questions truthfully?" The officer had a scruffy, deep voice. She was thin and short. Her hair was blonde and braided, and her eyes were green.

"Yes." I said solemnly.

"Where were you at roughly around seven o'clock in the evening on Monday, September 5?"

"I was resting at home, sitting on my backyard porch, and had a long smoke from my cigarette."

"Was Sakura with you?"

"No."

"Where was she?"

"I didn't know at the time, but when she came home she told me she had a doctor's appointment in Evernette."

"When did she leave to go there and when did she return?" I sat there, thinking for a few seconds.

"I'm not sure what time her appointment was, but it would have been between four and six. She came home about eleven-thirty."

"Has she told you anything else about where she went?"

"Yes. She was at that Safepath where a shooting took place. She was the one who stopped the bandits."

"Yeah, we've gathered that. Some witnesses told us she was involved. Anything else?"

"No."

"Where were you at three in the morning on Saturday, September 3?"

"I was sleeping at my house."

"And Sakura?"

"She spent the night. She moved in with me last week."

"Do you know Robby Samson?"

"Yes. He was a classmate."

"When was the last time you've had contact with him?"

"On Monday, around three to four in the afternoon."

"Where did you see him and what was happening?"

"I saw him at school near the wellness building. I asked him if he saw Sakura."

"What did he say?"

"He said that he didn't know where she was, but he talked to her earlier. And he said that he had a date with her at seven o'clock that night."

"Interesting," said the officer. "Looks like there's two possibilities. Sakura could have been in Evernette or with Robby."

"I don't think so. The shooting took place at that time and Sakura was there. So she wouldn't have been with Robby."

"You got me there. Okay. Do you know Sally Field?"

"Yes. She's also a classmate."

"You were involved in a fight with her, right?"

"Yes. There was a conflict between us."

"What was the basis of this argument?"

"Sally accused me and Sakura cheating with Robby. And she accused me of killing him."

"Why would she say that?"

"Because I was one of the last people who came in contact with him before his death."

"How did Sakura get involved?"

"She defended me when she saw us in the hallway. Then Sally challenged her to a fight."

"What's Sakura's relationship with Robby like?"

"Neutral. They're peers."

"So, they aren't dating?"

"No. They aren't close."

"Were you close with the young man?'

"No. Our relationship was neutral, too."

"Did you have a grudge against him, or any thoughts to hurt him?"

"No." I lied.

"There was a witness who told us that you threatened him on Monday. Is this true?"

"No, ma'am. We had a debate and he dared me to pull on his shirt if the argument lasted more than a minute, which it did. It might have seemed that I was threatening him, but I was not." I said this as convincingly as I possibly could.

"A debate? I thought you were asking about Sakura."

"I was. Then it led to the subject of animals with the largest reproductive organs." I explained.

"What a disturbed fellow," said the officer, disgusted. I nodded. "That very same witness who claimed that you threatened him said that you broke his nose."

"No. I didn't do that."

"Do you know who?"

"No, ma'am. I don't know." I lied.

"Do you have any idea who could have murdered Robby Samson or Mr. Ramsey Richard?"

"No, ma'am."

"When was the last time you saw Mr. Richard?"

"I last saw him in psychology class Friday morning."

"Did he tell you where he was going that evening or the next day?"

"No. He didn't."

"Have you ever been to his house, or at Robby's?"

"No, ma'am." The thought of ever going to their homes disturbed me. However, I concealed this sentiment with a focused, serious facial expression.

"Were you lying to me, or bent the truth on any of your answers during this session?"

"No, ma'am. I answered every question truthfully." I said confidently and stared at her straight in the eye. I knew I was a good liar and at that moment I felt proud about it. The woman turned off the tape recorder and dropped her pen on the notepad.

"Thank you for your cooperation, Miss Watson. We will give you a call if we need to talk with you again. You may leave." She motioned her hand to the door and led me outside. Sakura waited outside. The officer gave us a ride home.

CHAPTER TWENTY-NINE

I followed the female officer to an empty room. I sat across from her. She had a tape recorder, notepad, and pen. I felt nervous. She was large, muscular, and had strands of white hair growing out. She looked at me with her dark blue eyes and told me she was going to ask a few questions. She wanted me to answer them honestly.

"We're in the middle of a serious investigation. Two people are already dead, and it would be helpful if you cooperate with us, Miss Hatsukawa." I agreed to work with her.

"Where were you at three o'clock in the morning on Saturday?" she asked.

"At Jenna's. I was sleeping."

"When was the last time you saw Mr. Ramsey Richard?"

"I saw him after class on Friday. I needed to know if there was any make up work because I missed the first day of class."

"When did you last see or spoke to Robby Samson?"

"On Monday around two in the afternoon. I bumped into him near the wellness building."

"Did anything happen when you were there with him?"

"No. We just talked."

"We got a tip saying that you broke his nose. Is that true?"

"Yes. It was an accident. He wanted to know how to punch correctly. As I was demonstrating, he got too close to me and I hit him by accident."

"Someone saw him lying on the ground in pain and you ran off. What else happened?" I started to get nervous.

"That was also an accident. He wanted to know how to kick, so I showed him. Once again, he got so close that I unintentionally kicked him in the crotch. I asked if he was okay and he said he was fine and told me to go away. So, I ran off." I said this as calmly and articulately as I could.

"You were involved in the fight at Upgate Mall, correct?"

"Yes."

"What led to the conflict?"

"Sally Field was bullying my friend, Jenna. So, I came and defended Jenna. Then, Sally challenged me to a fight."

"Sally claimed that Jenna killed Robby."

"That's not true. Sally was jealous because Robby talked with Jenna when she didn't want him talking to her. Sally had a grudge on me because Robby liked me."

"Did you or Jenna liked Robby?"

"No. He's just a classmate."

"Did you go on a date with Robby that Monday evening?"

"No. I was in Evernette. I had a doctor's appointment and got stuck at that Safepath shooting."

"What time was the appointment?"

"Six o'clock that evening. I took the bus."

"What time did you get home?"

"By midnight."

"Did you take the bus back?"

"No. Someone offered me a ride."

"Who?"

"A woman I met at a bus stop that night. Her name was Cindy Hendricks."

"Is there a way we can reach her?"

"All I know is that she owns the hospital in Downtown."

"Do you know anyone who could have killed Robby Samson or Mr. Ramsey Richard?"

"No."

"Thank you for your time. You are dismissed."

CHAPTER THIRTY

"I'm going out of town tomorrow," said Sakura. I just got out of the bathroom, wrapped in a bath towel. My long hair was wet, and I smelled like lavender.

"What? Why?"

"It's my friend's birthday. Her name is Emi. Every year we spend it at her cabin in the Mountains."

"For how long?"

"A week. We go out camping, hang out at her cabin, and drive to Canada where she lives. It's the only week throughout the year when we see each other. She works as a model and she's always traveling." I searched my wardrobe and retrieved a pair of jeans and gray sweater.

"How old is she turning?" I inquired.

"Twenty-one."

"How did you meet her?"

"We've been friends since childhood. She lived across from me in Japan."

"Is she Japanese?"

"No. She's Irish and Canadian. Her parents lived in Japan for business purposes."

"Why didn't you tell me earlier?" I took off the towel and started dressing. Sakura watched me quietly and finally said something.

"Sorry. We canceled it at first because she couldn't make it, but she just called me and said she could after all."

I frowned, feeling a bit hurt. "I don't know if I'm ready to share you just yet."

"Come on now. It's not like I'm going to sleep with her," she stated.

"I know that. I'm just a bit unsure about the whole thing. Unexpected things could happen along the way. I don't want us to get separated because of it." I explained to her. I turned at her sadly in my bra and underwear. She moved her hand to my face and stroked my cheek gently and softly.

"Jenna, you'll always be my sweetheart. Emi and I are just friends. You and I are much more than that, love."

"I know. I just can't help but feel a little nervous and slightly jealous of this."

"I understand. I would feel the same way, too."

"So, I guess this means by tomorrow, I won't get to see your pretty face for a week."

"Don't worry, sweetie. I'll call you every day. I'll be back by next Monday."

"That's nice, but how about the wedding? It's on Saturday, but I leave on Wednesday."

"I wish I could come, but I guess I can't. Sorry."

"How about I give you a ride to the cabin? It's a long way from here, you know."

"No, it's fine. I'm meeting Emi in Dollard. She'll give me a lift there."

"Are you sure? I really don't mind giving you a ride, even to Dollard."

"No. Don't worry about it. Gas prices are high these days. Save some money babe."

I laughed and told her that saving money wasn't something all too necessary now. I pulled her close to me and looked into her alluring, beautiful eyes.

"Sakura," I said solemnly, "Give me a call if anything happens, okay? I'm going to miss you, and I'm going to be a bit worried. Have a fun time with your friend."

"Okay, Jenna. I promise. I'll miss you a lot, too. Don't worry so much. I will be okay." She offered to dress me up and do my hair as an excuse to spend quality time together. I quickly smiled and agreed.

CHAPTER THIRTY-ONE

"Sakura-chan!" Emi exclaimed with much excitement.

I ran into my childhood friend's arms and gave her a hug. After the hug, she looked at me from head to toe.

"Waa Sakura-chan! Kirei nee." ("Wow, Sakura! You're pretty!")

"Iee, mama desu. Demo Emi-chanwa totemo kireino." ("No, I'm average. But you are very pretty.")

"Of course!" She winked. "I am a model after all."

"That's right." I said. Emi worked as a model for the international modeling corporation and she travels to dozens of countries posing for several magazines.

"Let's get out of this town and go to my cabin," she said excitedly.

I walked with Emi in Dollard. The neighborhood was a friendly, Scandinavian area. We walked along Market Street where there were several shops and places to eat. We chatted endlessly. It was a year since I last saw her. She mentioned a lot about her numerous visits to several countries. Each story she told was enchanting. The drive in her black jeep was hours long, but we kept ourselves well occupied.

"So that's how I met him. His name's Luke. I even got his number. Man, do I love Paris!"

"That great! I'm glad you met someone."

"Yeah, and he's so hot. He's also novelist and quite the writer. How sexy is that?"

"How nice." I said.

"Are you seeing anyone, Sakura?"

"Yes." I said quickly.

"Who's the lucky gal? Does she treat you right? Let me know if she doesn't and I'll kick her ass for you." Emi was the only person whom I told my sexuality. We were close like sisters and I trusted her enough to tell her anything.

"She's lovely." I said reassuringly.

"Does she know you're with me all week?"

"Yes, she does. It's okay with her. She was uncertain at first, though."

"Yeah. I would too if my hot girlfriend was spending a whole week with some other chick. That's quite a situation, Sakura-chan."

"Emi, what do you know about dreams?"

"Not much. But they could have meaning. It depends I guess. Why?"

"I've been having strange dreams lately." She looked at me. Her light eyebrow lifted. She grew out her honey blonde hair. It reached the bottom of her abdomen. Her eyes were a deep blue color.

"Tell me about them. Maybe I can help you interpret." I told her the few dreams I've been having about the dark figure in a black hooded cloak.

"That's creepy. Maybe you know the killer? You know, the one that's been on the news lately that police are trying to find. Maybe the hooded cloak person symbolizes the killer."

"Maybe."

"Or maybe…" she paused.

"Or what?" I looked at her. She stared at me coldly with her deep blue eyes.

"Maybe they're back," she said.

"What are you talking about?"

"Your visions."

"No way. It can't be. I haven't had those since I was a kid."

"I know, but it's a possibility."

"I don't even want to think about it. That was long ago."

"Not really. It's only been a decade ago."

"I know. But ever since I ignored my power, I lost it. I can't believe this." I buried my face in my hands.

"Sakura, you can't deny your gift. Man, I wish I could have such power. I would use it to my advantage."

"It's not all that great, really. It's actually quite a burden."

"I can understand that. But think about it. You were chosen, Sakura. God or the Universe has given you this power so make the best of it. You just need to learn to accept it and not let it get the best of you."

"All I want to be is normal."

"'Normal' varies for each person. But you're normal to me. Don't worry about it. It's not like people can recognize the fact that you could foresee the future or the past by looking at you."

"Thank goodness for that." I sighed in relief.

We finally arrived at Emi's cabin in the Mountains early that evening. It was situated near a river, deep within the woods. It was the best place to get away from the noisy city. We sat at the fireplace and had a toast for her twenty-first birthday.

"So how do you feel? I can't wait until I'm your age." I said.

"I don't feel any different. And don't be eager to grow up fast. You only have one chance being twenty. After that you cannot be twenty again."

"I know. I'm just the type to of person who's always thinking ahead into the future."

"Just focus on the present and enjoy it."

"I will." I promised.

"Good."

"When did you come to town?"

"Not too long ago. I arrived here on the fifth. It's been about two weeks now. I've heard about those killings. I wonder who it is."

"Yeah. My girlfriend and I were suspects."

"Seriously?"

"Yup."

"Yikes. That's scary."

"It is."

"Did the police question you?"

"Yeah. Yesterday."

"I bet you were nervous."

"Oh, I was. Very."

"I don't think I can drive to Canada anytime this week."

"Why not? We always do."

"My cousins there are staying over there for the week while their homes are being repaired. There was an arson."

"Did they find out who the arsonist was?"

"Yeah. And that guy is going to pay big time."

"That's terrible, Emi. I hope everything works out okay."

"Thanks. I'm sure things will be fine, eventually," she said reassuringly.

"I'm tired." I said. I yawned loudly.

"Me too. Let's hit the sack. Tomorrow we can go hiking."

"Sounds good to me."

I lie awake at the bottom bunk bed staring out the window. It was a cold, windy night. The river nearby flowed quickly and its waves rippled fast. Across the river was a timber wolf. It howled, sending shivers up my spine. I closed my eyes, trying to drift to sleep, but I kept hearing a voice whisper through the wind: "It has come for you. You mustn't stay here for long."

I hid myself under the covers. I could hear footsteps a few feet away. I peered through the sheets and that's when I saw her. A little girl with brown eyes stared at me, motioning me to follow her. Her hair was short and black. On her chest was a stain of blood dripping on her white skin. She wore a green dress with matching shoes. I recognized her. She was Lisa Thompson, the same girl who was shot a few days ago at the mall. I slowly got out of bed and followed her outside. We sat on the doorstep. I pinched myself, making sure that I wasn't dreaming.

"You are the only one that can stop it," she said. Her voice was soft and low as a whisper.

"What is it that you're talking about?"

"The vampire. Only you can stop it."

"How?"

"You know."

"No. I don't."

"Then you'll find out soon."

"Who is it?"

"You already know." I stared at her, blankly.

"You met the vampire several times. It's very fond of you."

"Who? Will you tell me?"

"You will find out soon. Be careful. You are the only one that can weaken and destroy it."

"Who sent you?"

"The Universe."

"Why me?"

"You were chosen."

"I've heard."

"It's true."

"Aren't you dead?"

"Yes. I died last night at the hospital. Mommy can't stop crying. I feel bad."

"Don't. It's not your fault nor your mother's fault. You didn't make it happen"

"But I am her only child and she can't conceive again because she has cancer."

"I'm sorry to hear that."

"My name's Lisa. I admire you very much. You fought well with Sally." I looked down at her and lifted my eyebrow.

"You shouldn't admire me. I'm not all too proud of my fighting skills. Sometimes I wish I didn't know martial arts."

"I can tell you are a good person. That's why I like you." She smiled.

"How is it like to die?" I asked. I was curious.

"When you're about to cross over, you forget about time. Your whole life flashes before your eyes and you quickly evaluate it. I was in a tunnel and at the very end of it was bright light. As I walked towards it. Then I was told that I'm not quite finished in this world. I had to go back and warn you about the vampire. I was sent to watch over you, Sakura."

"You mean to tell me that you're my guardian angel?"

"Yes. I am."

"Aren't you a bit young?"

"Age is irrelevant when you're dead. Anyone can be a guardian angel."

"I guess. I just find all this hard to believe."

"Well, what you see is what you get. Believe it or not, I am here for you."

The wolf across the river jumped over the stream and walked towards us. Lisa petted it. It licked her hand and lied down beside her.

"Who's this?" I asked.

"This is Malto. He will be your companion, too."

"Is he dead like you?"

"Yes. He was a hero when he was alive. He helped obtain antibiotics to a little, remote town a hundred years ago."

"Hi Malto." I said. I patted his head. He wagged his tall and licked my cheek. Its neck was covered with blood. I asked Lisa what happened to him.

"A vampire attacked him after he tried to chase a thief."

"I think I dreamt of the attack. I dreamt I was the thief."

"Your dreams aren't ordinary."

"Tell me about it. They scare the hell out of me."

"Your dreams are either premonitions or visions. You must stop the vampire until it strikes again. There shouldn't be any more deaths in town. And he likes you." She pointed at Malto.

"How can I touch him if he's dead?"

"Because he allowed you to."

"So, I'm the only one who can see you guys, huh."

"Yes. You can see the dead. It's a special ability. Didn't you know that?"

"Of course. I just ignored it for years."

"You shouldn't do that. They might need your help."

"I know. Thanks for the advice."

"That's why I'm here."

CHAPTER THIRTY-TWO

I sat contentedly on my seat. The plane flew high in the air and the sun shined through the small window. I looked down at the ground. The buildings, cars, and people looked like ants. It was amazing how lovely an aerial view of the city could be. I was in for a long flight. I didn't understand why we had to fly towards the Pacific if we could simply fly through the Atlantic Ocean. A small television screen hung above the seat in front of me. I spent most of the air travel asleep. I didn't know why, but whenever I flew, it made me sleepy.

I had an issue with the man sitting next to me because he was singing loudly as he listened to his ipod. He was a short, large, bold guy with a terrible singing voice. Whenever he tried to sing, he ended sounded like an elephant and bellowed loudly. I tapped on his shoulder, but it seemed that he did not felt it. He continued singing. I removed his earphones. He finally noticed that someone sat next to him. He didn't look pleased at all to see me.

"Oye! I was listening to that, you know," he scolded. He had a Scottish accent.

"I'm sorry to disturb you, sir. But you're singing much too loud. Could you listen to your ipod quietly, please? I'm trying to sleep." I explained.

"If you pay me."

"What?"

"You heard me. Pay me and I'll stop singing."

"I will not!" I grew angry.

"Then I will sing."

"I'll tell the attendant that you're disturbing a passenger." I threatened.

"See if I care," he said bitterly. Then he continued to sing. A teenage boy sitting an aisle across from us threw a package of peanuts at the man's head. The noisy man got up and started arguing with the boy. A male flight attendant came over and broke up the fight.

"Sir, please go back to your seat," said the flight attendant politely.

"I can't sit there. That woman doesn't want me to." I explained the situation to the attendant.

"Sir. You can't be loud on the plane. Please go back to your seat and be quiet." The large, bold, Scottish man bitterly obeyed and returned to his spot. He listened to his ipod in silence the rest of the way.

I couldn't wait to get home. I haven't seen mum or Gregory in nearly four years and I missed them. I was happy for mum because ever since she and daddy got divorced a year after their marriage, she was depressed. I did everything I could as a kid to help her cope with it, but nothing seemed to work. She would lock herself in her bedroom for hours late at night when she thought I was sleeping. She spent those many long hours in solitude, crying. I felt sorry for mum. I couldn't wait to see her happy face when she walks along the church aisle. She was now an old woman and someone as loving as her deserves to live the rest of her life happily with another person who would take good care of her.

I pulled my ipod out of my purse and listened to a variety of genres from opera, jazz, and hip-hop. I managed to fall asleep when my favorite song played. It was a slow, beautiful, soothing song that put me my mind at ease and helped me fall asleep.

CHAPTER THIRTY-THREE

On Thursday Emi and I swam in the lake that was a few minutes away from the cabin. I was in my blue bikini and she decided to go skinny-dipping.

"Why are you in your bikini?" she asked. She took off the remaining clothing she wore, tossed it on a large rock, and jumped in the water with me.

"I should be the one asking you why in the world are you going to swim naked." I retorted.

"Very funny."

"The water's cold, Emi."

"So? I like it better that way," she said apathetically.

"I'd rather cover at least my most tender parts just in case someone comes along and takes a dip."

"Like that's going to happen," she snorted.

"You never know." I said.

"No one else is around here within miles so I'm taking the liberty to do as I wish. You should try it out sometime. It's a lot more fun as a group."

"I'm sure it is." I said sarcastically.

Emi dived under the water and pinched my leg. Startled, I jumped. I splashed her when she surfaced and not before long, we were having a splashing fight. I haven't had such fun since I was a kid.

We spent the evening roasting marshmallows at her fireplace. Emi asked me if I've been having weird dreams since we arrived at the cabin.

"Yeah. But they're vague. I hardly remember them." I said.

"I'm sure you remember enough to tell me what they were about."

"Not really." I lied. In fact, my dreams were quite vivid. The other night I dreamt I was in a jail cell. I felt weak and starved. I wanted to get out so badly that I cried and hollered at the guards until they came and mocked me. They took me to an empty white room and strapped me to the padded wall in a stretcher.

I closed my eyes and stopped my breathing. The nurse came in to check up on me. She was surprised that I was motionless. She untangled me and laid me on the ground. When she found out I had no pulse, she got up and headed towards the locked door. I immediately stood up, grabbed the nurse, and sealed her mouth to prevent her from screaming. I took out a needle from her breast pocket and used it one her. Within seconds, the woman fell asleep. I swapped clothes with her, thankful that they fit me. I slyly moved through the building. No one ever questioned my presence. I left the building, stole a car, and drove aimlessly through the streets.

My cell phone rang. I answered it. It was Jenna.

"Hey sweetie," I said. Emi sat quietly, listening.

"Hey baby. How are you?" She spoke in a thick Australian accent. I could hardly recognize her when she spoke.

"I'm fine dear. How are you?"

"Great. I just arrived in Perth."

"What time is it there?"

"It's two in the afternoon. It should be in evening there, right?" I checked my watch. She was right.

"Yeah. It's almost eleven here. You must be fifteen hours ahead, huh."

"Yes."

"I miss you." I said.

"I miss you, too love. I've thought a lot about you."

"Me too." I smiled. I had a feeling she was smiling, too.

"So, what are you up to? Is Emi there? Tell her I said hi."

"I will. We're roasting marshmallows over the fireplace."

"Sounds delicious."

"It is."

"I wish I could have some."

"Maybe we could make some of our own next week." I suggested.

"Brilliant idea, sweetie."

"Yup."

"Did you hear that Sally broke out of jail?"

"What?" I was shocked.

"She escaped and she's on the loose. The police are frantically searching for her." Just then I remembered the dream I had a few nights ago.

"That's creepy. Where do think she's heading?" I asked.

"I don't know, but I thought you should know all of this. Be careful, Sakura. If I hear anything fishy going on over there, I'm going to fly back and check it out myself. I'll let you know if anything comes up over here."

"I will. You be careful over there, too. Have a fun time, but not too much fun, if you know what I mean." She giggled.

"Don't worry, sweetness. I wouldn't dare screw around with another woman because you're the only one I've got, and ever want."

"That's nice to hear, love. Thank you."

"You're welcome."

Emi asked me how Jenna and I met after I got off the phone. I told her the entire story that luckily brought us together. Emi was enthralled by the tale. She took a sip of booze and told me that perhaps it was fate that brought us together. I insisted it was pure coincidence.

"But if you haven't bumped into her, then you might still be at the hospital recovering from a concussion."

"I guess it was a good thing that I woke up late that day."

"Yeah. And it's nice that she arrived tardy, too. What a lovely story, Sakura-chan."

"Thanks, Emi-chan."

Emi ended up sleeping on the sofa as I spent the rest of the night on the carpet with a large pillow. I had a blanket covering me and so did Emi. The fire slowly dwindled to a tiny spark until there wasn't anything left.

CHAPTER THIRTY-FOUR

I pulled my luggage and stood in the humid airport, searching for mum through the crowd. I spotted her after a few minutes. She wore a bright, orange summer dress, white sandals, and a large, beige sunhat. I was perspiring in my black sweater and jeans. Mum ran up to me and embraced me. She was almost sixty, but she looked twenty years younger. Her blue eyes smiled when she saw me. Her short hair still glimmered red and her skin was visibly unwrinkled.

"Jenna, you look fabulous," she said.

"Mum, you look wonderful, too." I kissed her cheek. I followed her outside where Gregory waited patiently in the white minivan. He was sixty-two, but like mum, he appeared to be younger. He seemed like fifty and not a strand of gray hair could be traced on him. I don't know how they both do it.

"Hi, Jen. Good to see you again. Long time no see," he said. He wore a white suit with matching black shoes. He looked as if he were attending a ball. He handed me a pink rose.

"Thank you, Greg. This is very lovely. It's nice to see you, too." I threw my entire luggage in the trunk and sat in the back seat. Mum sat up front with her fiancé.

"So, where's your friend? I thought she was coming," said mum. Gregory's eyes were glued to the road as he drove.

"She had to go someplace else for the week."

"Where's she now?" asked mum.

"She's back in Washeendom. She's in the Mountains on a trip with a friend." I explained.

"I see. And you weren't invited?"

"I couldn't come along, mum. I wouldn't want to miss this occasion for the world, you know." She turned to me and smiled warmly.

"I'm very happy you came, dear."

"We both are," added Gregory. We drove the rest of the way in silence.

Mum and Gregory owned a beach house in town. The house was white and three stories high with an outdoor spa. Gregory offered to carry my things as mum guided me to a room. It was my bedroom I had as a kid. Mum did nothing to change it over the years. She left it completely untouched. I placed my luggage on the twin bed. The walls to my old bedroom were baby blue. I had posters of animals scattered on the walls. Most of them were of wild felines and wolves, which were my favorite animals. I opened the closet near the doorway and pulled out a pink dress I wore when I was eight. My fingers ran through the polyester fabric. I sniffed the dress and realized it smelled like honey.

I saw a photo album on my desk I used to study at. I picked it up and flipped through the pages. Many of the pictures were of mum and me. The last picture was taken outside at the beach. My first girlfriend and I sat together in the sand in our bikinis, holding hands and smiled at the camera. Her name was Jessica Munson. The picture was taken when we were fifteen. The door to the room slowly opened and a tall, slender woman entered. She wore a green tank top and white shorts with purple sandals. Her hair was short and white blonde. Her skin was tanned, and her eyes were hazel.

"Jessica?" I said to her. She looked almost the same when I left years ago.

"Welcome back, Jenna." she said and walked up to me. She took my hand and kissed my lips.

"I missed you very much, Jen," she whispered. "We have a lot of catching up to do."

"Yes, we do. But as friends." I emphasized the "friend" part. I wiped my lips with my sleeve.

"But didn't we have something great? We were wonderful together. Don't you love me anymore?"

"I like you, but only as a friend. Nothing more. And we broke up a long time ago. Things weren't going all too well, you know."

"What do you mean?" She looked at me sadly.

"We were young back then and we didn't know any better, Jess. My head was in the clouds and our relationship didn't have much depth. I was only in it for the excitement and late nights. I'm older now and I'm not quite up for that stuff anymore. I want to settle."

"Then settle here with me. I want to be with you, Jen."

"No. I can't do that."

"Why not?" She stroked my face. I pulled back away from her.

"I'm seeing someone else. That's why." I said. Jessica frowned and folded her arms across her chest.

"Who is she?" she asked seriously.

"Her name's Sakura. I met her recently in Washeendom."

"You're with a Japanese girl?"

"Yes. She's also Filipina and Spanish."

"I thought you only liked Australian or English girls." she said, confused.

"I don't know where you heard that, but I like a variety of women." I said firmly.

"What does she have that I don't?" she asked irritably.

"You wouldn't understand."

"What do you mean?"

"By that I mean I don't want to explain it to you."

"Come on. Tell me. What makes her more special than me?"

"Why do you ask too many questions?" I was getting annoyed.

"I'm just curious."

"Well, I've got to get my things organized. I'll talk to you later."

"You're getting rid of me? How rude! This conversation isn't over." She stomped out of my room, slamming the door behind her.

I washed the dishes for mum when the front doorbell rang. Gregory answered it and called for me. I left the kitchen and walked over to the living room. Jessica was standing on the doorstep. Gregory left us alone.

"What are you doing here?" I asked her.

"Aren't you happy to see me? I feel like I'm not appreciated anymore, Jen." She said hurtfully.

"I'm sorry." I said tiredly.

"What's wrong? You aren't very cheery."

"I know. I'm not in the best mood now."

"I see," Jessica said sympathetically.

"Anyway, how've you been?"

"Good. It can get better if you come with me," she said.

"Where?"

"Dancing. Let's go out and dance. Just like old times. My treat."

"I'm a bit tired." I said.

"That's a lame excuse," she retorted.

"I just arrived here. I don't think I'm ready for too much excitement on my first night."

"Come on, Jen. I bet that flight was boring. And you can never have too much excitement. Come and have a fun girls' night out. Connie and Roxanne are waiting in the car. You love to dance." she insisted. Connie and Roxanne were her two close friends. Like me, Connie was a blue-eyed dark redhead that looked brunette. Unfortunately, she was a major alcoholic. Roxanne was a green-eyed black-haired woman with glasses who often goes out for one-night stands. I wasn't surprised she brought her both of her party animals along.

"Well, the thought of dancing, music, and drinks does sound tempting. And I haven't gone to a club in a long time." I said.

"Great. Let's go." She took my hand and started running to her car. I pulled back.

"Aren't you coming?" she asked.

"Yes. Hold on. I have to tell mum." I hurried inside and told mum I would be back late. She told me to have a good time. I promised her that I would.

"Okay, let's go," said Jessica.

CHAPTER THIRTY-FIVE

Emi and I sat on top of the grassy hill outside the cabin and gazed at the sky. I saw a cluster of stars shaped like a UFO. I pointed at it and told my friend. She said that it did look just like a UFO and she pointed at one that looked like a unicorn. I agreed with her finding. This was what I liked about places outside the city. They came with fine evening scenery.

"I love it here," said Emi.

"It's nice, but I'm used to the city." I commented.

"I know. You and your city-dwelling tastes."

"How long have you had the lodge?"

"Ever since my parents came and settled here years ago."

"Have you gone back to Ireland?" I asked.

"No. Not in a long time. I was three-years-old when I left."

"And you don't remember anything?"

"Nope. My family there was poor, and my parents thought it was best if we didn't live there anymore. They thought a poor environment wouldn't be good for my development."

"You can still be a great person and come from a poor family background, Emi."

"I know, but my parents thought differently."

"Yeah. Many do."

"Tell me more about you and your girlfriend," she said.

"What do you want to know?"

"Lots. Give me the dirt."

"We haven't done much aside from kissing and cuddling."

"That's it? You just swapped saliva and held each other? Wow. I thought you did more by now."

"I'm sure that'll happen when the right time comes."

"Were you ever tempted to go further?"

"Of course. Many times. I just wasn't ready."

"I know how that can be. It's best if you're relaxed and you fantasize doing her at the same time. It works much better that way." I lifted my eyebrow.

"What makes you such an expert?" I questioned her.

"I have my share of romances, pal." She winked at me.

"That's right. You're a model. I bet you slept with several men, huh."

"I've slept with a few here and there. Casual hook ups. Some of them wanted to negotiate and made advanced onto me, but I preferred not to play games like that. No matter how much I could easily excel in this career by sleeping with certain guys. I refuse to sell my body like that. My body isn't just for any dude. It's my own first."

"That's true. I just don't like that this is a reality."

"I know. The truth can suck, and life can be a pain in the ass."

"Yeah." I agreed.

CHAPTER THIRTY-SIX

We arrived at the club at ten that Friday evening. I was dressed in a black tank top with matching black pants and red shoes. I tied my long hair back, so it wouldn't get in the way of my dancing. Jessica wore a silver, tight outfit that showed a bit of cleavage. Connie had on a navy-blue sports bra and black shorts. Roxanne was dressed as a red and white striped cheerleader outfit.

"You should have brought along pon pons." I told Roxanne.

"I know. But I didn't have any. This outfit will do," she said.

The four of us danced in the crowd. The room stank with sweat, booze, and perfume. I danced solo in my own little space as the other three women were doing the freak train. Jessica motioned me to come and join them, but I stayed where I was. I felt a finger tap my shoulder. I turned around and there stood my old childhood friend, Marvin.

"Jenna Watson? Is that you?" He looked at me.

"Marvin Ramsey. How's it going?" I patted him on the shoulder. He was a big and buff guy. He lifted weights ever since he was ten and he has become a professional body builder. He was tan and had spiked, bleached, blonde hair with white streaks. His eyes were light brown and he looked quite attractive.

"Pretty good, mate. How you been? Haven't seen you in years, Jen."

"Been in Washeendom for school."

"Riveting."

"Yes."

"When did you come?"

"Today."

"How long are you staying?"

"A few days. I'll leave on Sunday," I responded. Jessica walked up to us.

"Well, if it isn't Marvin." she said.

"Hey, Jess." he greeted.

"What are you up to?" Jessica asked.

"Nothing much. Came here to meet some fine ladies." He winked. Jessica laughed. I left them both and slowly made my way to the restroom.

I washed my face and brushed my messy hair. My makeup was smeared all over my face and I found it irritating because it wasn't too long ago that I had applied some on. I could hear the loud techno music playing outside and I smelled strongly of booze and cigarette smoke. I applied more lavender perfume on myself, hoping the awful stench would go away. I went to one of the stalls and locked the door.

I sat on the toilet to urinate. When I flushed it, I couldn't help but smell a rotten fowl scent coming from the stall next to mine. I opened the door to see if anyone was inside, but it was locked. I looked underneath and saw a pair of bare feet. I slid my head beneath the stall and saw a dead woman sitting on the toilet seat. Her pink dress was torn and covering in dirt. Her neck was pierced, and her skin was completely pale. I screamed, ran back to the toilet, and vomited. I ran out the restroom and told the club workers my discovery. They went over to look for themselves. When they returned, their faces were green. They announced that the club had to be shut down until further notice. Everyone, including my friends complained. However, they all obediently left the building. Jessica drove Connie and I home. Roxanne went home with Marvin. I tiptoed upstairs to my room, so I wouldn't wake up mum or Gregory. I fell asleep by midnight. I set my alarm at eight, which was three hours before the wedding started.

The wedding turned out beautifully. It took place outside on a grassy cliff. The weather was typical: sunny and warm. I sat in the front row of white chairs and watched the ceremony from beginning to end. Mum was beautifully dressed in a large, fancy, traditional, white wedding gown. I noticed that it was the same dress she wore at her first wedding with daddy. Gregory looked dashing in his black tuxedo.

They walked down the aisle, hand in hand until they met with the priest. It was a lovely event. The entire time I visualized my wedding with Sakura. The both of us would be dressed up so beautifully. I yearned for that day to come so that she and I would always together as one. There was a party afterwards. I drank a lot of punch and talked endlessly to numerous people whom I haven't met before. Many of them were Gregory's relatives and handfuls more were mum's friends.

"You must be Elizabeth's daughter," an elderly woman said to me. She wore a pink dress with matching sandals and had on a sunhat. I realized aside from mum and I, all the women had on sunhats. I kind of felt out of place since practically everyone was years older than me. Fortunately, everybody was very friendly and polite.

"Yes. I'm Jenna." I introduced myself. "It's nice to meet you."

"It's a pleasure to get acquainted with you, Jenna," said the woman. "My name is Lucy. I'm Gregory's older sister. I guess this means you're my niece."

"I guess so." I said.

"Anyhow, it was nice meeting you. Excuse me while I run to the john," said Lucy.

"Okay." The event lasted for hours and by late afternoon, mum, Gregory, and I headed home.

"Too bad your father couldn't come, Jenna," said mum.

"Yes. I was hoping he'd show up."

"You know how busy of a man he is, being a doctor and all that." Daddy was tall, handsome and intelligent. He had dark brown hair and bright blue eyes. He would be the same age as mum, but like her, he looked a lot younger. I was proud of him.

"Maybe he'll call later tonight," said Gregory.

"I hope so. I haven't spoken to him in a long time." I thought.

Daddy called my cell phone later that evening.

"Jenna? Is that you?" he asked. His voice was just the way I remembered it growing up: soft and soothing.

"Yes, daddy." I said.

"Baby, I'm so sorry for not showing up at the wedding this morning. I had an urgent operation."

"I know, daddy. Mum told me everything."

"She did? Was she upset?"

"No. We understand. Really."

"Well, that's nice to hear. Now things are a bit calmer."

"Good."

"So, how's everything for you? Are you leaving Australia soon?"

"Everything is fine, daddy. I leave tomorrow morning."

"Tell your mother and her new husband that I said hello."

"I will. Have you been seeing anyone lately?"

"No, love. I've been way too busy to date."

"You should go out sometime. Take a break from work and enjoy yourself." I advised him. Daddy was always so serious when it comes to his work. That's the reason why he and mum separated. He never could make time for family or himself. He was a great provider though. He was an honest, kind man. I loved him a lot. Sometimes I wish they hadn't divorced so I could have seen him whenever I came to visit mum.

"I'll try, princess. Hey, why don't you come over here and visit me sometime? I want to spend some time with my favorite daughter."

"I'm you're only daughter." I reminded him.

"That's right. You're my only kid. So how about it? I want to see you."

"Can I invite a friend?"

"Who?"

"Her name is Sakura. She and I are really close."

"Sure. The more the merrier. I haven't been around young ladies in ages." I laughed.

"Okay, daddy. When's a good day for you?"

"How about next week? Come by on Saturday when you can. I scheduled the weekend off."

"Are you sure? And you won't cancel it?"

"I promise. Cross my heart."

"Okay, daddy. I'm excited."

"Me too, Jen," he said enthusiastically.

I hung up and went outside to sit on the front porch. Mum and Gregory left to go on their honeymoon a few miles away at a cozy hotel. They would be back early before I leave. I sat alone and smoked a cigarette. The fumes rose in the sky. The night was warm and dry. That's the overall climate of the country. My body couldn't handle it the first day, but soon afterwards I adjusted to it. I loved my home here. It was surrounded by water and warm weather. I couldn't believe I've spent my childhood growing up in Perth and in Sheffield.

It's incredible how much time passes by. One day you're young and curious. The next day you're an adult and serious. I sat on the porch, reminiscing my childhood memories. All those days I skipped down the beach in Perth and scraped my knees on the ground in England. All those days I ran and played cricket with friends. All those days I swam in the lake in my bathing suit and had picnics with mum. All those days when daddy carried me on his shoulders at the park and walked my Dalmatian, Sammy. All those days seemed vivid in my mind. I could almost touch the ground I walked on or breathe the air. However, they were just memories, time capsules of events that I hope to never forget.

Jessica walked by and saw me at the porch. She came and sat next to me.

"Good evening," she said.

"Good evening."

"Are you leaving tomorrow?" she asked.

"Yes." I took another drag from my cigarette.

She showed me her palm, a gesture meaning to pass the cigarette. I shared mine with her. She took it and slowly breathed into it, relishing as much as she could of it.

"We've had a rough start and I'm sorry for being the one that started the argument," she said.

"No hard feelings." I told her.

"Thanks. But I still have strong feelings for you, Jen."

"I know. But that's in the past."

"Yeah. That girlfriend of yours is very lucky. I wish you two the best in your relationship." I smiled at her.

"You really mean that, Jess?"

"Of course. I want you to be happy."

She turned to me and looked into my eyes. Her eyes were one of the chief reasons as to why I fell in love with her. They shimmered even in the dark. The other reasons were her spontaneous sexual actions along with her willingness to try new things and act extremely adventurous. She took my hand and held it. I allowed her to, for I would be departing the next day. We probably won't see each other until years later.

"Thanks, Jess. I'll miss you."

"Really?"

"Yes. You've been a good friend to me all these years. And you'll always remain as a good friend to me." I smiled at her. She smiled back and softly kissed my cheek.

"Can I ask for a favor, please?" she whispered.

"What is it?" I asked.

"Can I have one last kiss? A real one?"

I hesitated a few moments. The thought of kissing her would make me feel guilty since I promised Sakura I wouldn't screw around. However, I would consider it merely a slight momentary approach, so I finally agreed. I leaned forward and kissed her lips. Jessica wrapped her arms around my neck and held me tightly. Both our eyes were closed. I started to feel heated and tingly. I could tell that she wanted to go further because she started sliding her hand down my back and along my sides, so I broke the kiss before anything else could happen. I made a vow to Sakura to resist such crazy temptation.

"I felt a spark for a while," she said. She hung her head hung low to make her blushing less noticeable. "Did you feel it, too?"

"A little bit. If I were single, I would have probably gone farther with you, but I can't. I hope you understand."

"I know." She stroked my cheek and kissed it one last time before leaving.

CHAPTER THIRTY-SEVEN

Emi and I were driving back to the city. It was Monday morning and I was excited to see Jenna again.

"So, did you have a good time?" asked Emi.

"Yeah. I did. Thanks for having me over."

"Hey, it was great. I haven't had that much fun in a long time. I look forward to next year's get together."

I investigated the side mirror to fix my hair when a little girl appeared in the back seat, along with her canine companion. It was Lisa and Malto. I froze, ignored my reflection and stared at them from the mirror.

"Be careful when you drive," she warned. "It's coming after Emi." Malto nodded and barked in agreement. Then they both disappeared.

"*What do they mean?*" I asked myself. I was confused and scared. Emi saw my frightened face.

"Anything wrong?" she asked concernedly.

"No." I lied. I knew she didn't believe me, so I made up a response that she would take seriously. "Just had a vision last night."

"What was it?"

I took a deep breath. "Your death." I said. She turned pale.

"Just watch the road." I told her.

Emi drove cautiously, her eyes glued to the window. It began to rain hard. The roar of thunder could be heard from the distance. I turned on the window wipers. Emi turned on the radio. Just then, a deer appeared. Emi swerved along the road to dodge the animal, but it ran in the same direction. She stepped on the breaks, but we hit it.

"Oh my God! We killed it," shrieked Emi. She started to panic. I stepped outside and looked at the creature. It was dead. I heard heavy footsteps in the distance. I turned around and saw a dark figure walking fast towards us. A violent lighting struck it. The figure got electrocuted and collapsed to the ground. I thought it was dead, so I started walking towards it. Emi was calling me, but her voice was heavily droned from the thunder. As I got closer to the mysterious being in black, it started to move. Before I knew it, the figure was standing a few feet away from me. Its face was well hidden in its cloak, but its yellow eyes glowed radiantly. It bared its fangs and smiled roguishly. I looked down at its feet and noticed it was levitating. My jaw dropped. I ran back to the jeep. I jumped into the passenger seat and slammed the door hard. Emi was startled by my hastiness.

"Hit the gas! Forget about the deer." I commanded.

"Why?" she asked. She turned around and saw the figure quickly approaching.

"Holy shit! What is that thing?" she said.

"Just drive!" I screamed. We drove fast along the abandoned road, aimlessly following its path.

"What the hell was that?" asked Emi. It finally disappeared in the distance.

"The thing in my dreams. It's responsible for all the killings."

"Shit," she muttered.

"No kidding." I said. "Emi, listen. That thing was after you."

"What? Why?"

"I don't know why, but I know because someone told me."

"Who?"

"A dead girl. She's the same girl that got shot at the Upgate mall."

"Wait a minute, you can see dead people now?"

"I always could, but I ignored them growing up."

"Jeez. That's crazy. Why didn't tell me?"

"I thought you'd think I was crazy."

"Well, I believed your visions, so I wouldn't be surprised if you could see dead people."

"I'm sorry. I was just afraid of your reaction."

"You didn't have to hide it from me or lie about it, Sakura."

"I know. Sorry."

"It's fine. So that thing was really after me, huh."

"Yeah."

"Then what the hell do I do when it tries to bite me?"

"I don't know. I'm not sure what its weakness is."

"Fuck. Let me know what it is before I die," she said sarcastically.

"I'll figure it out somehow. Then I'll let you know right away."

CHAPTER THIRTY-EIGHT

I arrived home Monday morning to an empty house. Before my departure, I gave mum a long hug and shook Gregory's hand. I was tired and hungry when I got back. I unpacked my belongings, put them away, and searched the refrigerator for grub. I quietly ate leftover tofu, vegetables, and steamed rice. Then I took a long nap on the sofa.

I woke up to the doorbell ringing. I got up, stretched my stiff back, and opened the door. It was Sakura. She was completely soaked. I carried her items to the bedroom as she took off her wet jacket. Then she put away all her belongings.

"How was your trip with Emi?" I asked.

"It was a lot of fun. I wish you could have come." Sakura continued putting her belongings away.

"I know. Maybe I'll come along next year."

"That would be great. How was the wedding? How are your folks?"

"It was lovely, thanks. You should have been there. My folks are doing fine. I thought about our own marriage at the ceremony." I explained. Sakura blushed. I asked why she reddened.

"I never thought about marriage before. It would a be nice event I guess."

"I'm not a huge believer in marriage, but the thought of being engaged to someone like you blows my mind away." I started daydreaming about the special day.

"Why aren't you a believer of marriage?" she asked.

"Because I don't think you need a piece of paper, legal confirmation, or special ceremony to prove your love to someone or seal a lifetime union. However, I guess having a wedding would be fun. It gives us an excuse to dress up lovely and have all our families happily gather together and celebrate."

"Married or not, Jenna, you know that I love you very much."

"I know, and I'm such a lucky lady." I smiled.

When she was done getting settled, I couldn't help myself. I ran up to her and kissed her hard. My arms encircled her firmly. She held me tightly, one hand behind my head as the other situated on my back. My clothes got wet from hers, but I could care less. She broke the kiss and whispered in my ear how much she missed me. I told her I craved to be with her every night when we were apart. She kissed me passionately and touched my waist, stroking my sides.

I broke the kiss and told her, "I wish to make love to you someday. When you are ready." She kissed my lips and whispered in my ear, "I am. I want you now. I'm also in the mood. Let's do it." I felt thrilled and eager to give pleasure and make love. I kissed her passionately. She tugged on her clothing and beckoned me to undress her.

Slowly removing her clothes, I guided us to our bed. I stripped off her shirt and began kissing her chest. She guided my hands to her back for me to unhook her bra. I removed her bra and threw it on the bed as I continued kissing her bare chest. I sucked on one of her nipples as I gentle massaged and tweaked the other. She moaned softly as I resumed doing it. I moved my lips down her breasts and licked her belly button. She stroked my hair and moaned softly again, pleased by my action. My hands wandered along her upper body to caress her bosoms. She whispered that we continued in the shower. I agreed.

Our lips never left each other as we erratically transitioned to the bathroom. When we reached the doorway, she slowly unbuttoned her jeans as I helped pull them down. I ran my hand down her legs, feeling her soft, moist skin until her pants were completely off.

She was wearing only her underwear when she started to undress me. I watched memorized by her warm, soft hands as they took my top off. She had an intriguing smile when doing this and kissed my neck softly as she took off my pants. Her hands ran upward from my ankles to my inner thighs where she caressed my crotch in a circular motion with increased pressure. I breathed deeply and exhaled a soft moan when she did that. She kissed my lips passionately and circled her arms around my back to unclip my bra. My bra dropped to the floor. Her hands glided all over my torso and cupped my breasts and squeezed them. We both were wearing only our panties.

My hands and lips explored as much of her as I possibly could along the way to the shower. She giggled when I removed her last garment: her white panties. She turned on the shower and took off my underwear with her teeth. So cheeky. It was such a sensual feeling being with her like this. I felt so turned on and ready to give pleasure to her in the way she desired.

By the time we were both naked, all our clothes were scattered on the bathroom and bedroom floor. I sucked on her soft, slender neck as she breathed heavily. She ran her hands up and down my back and squeezed my buttocks. I loved it when she did that. I whispered to her how much I enjoyed that grasp. She giggled and gave my buttocks a light spank, which felt good to me. I began nibbling on her neck when she suddenly dug her fingernails on my back. I couldn't feel the slight pain in all the passion.

"I want to do naughty things to you, Sakura. I crave for you. I'm addicted to you. Baby, I want you." I whispered in her ear and resumed licking her neck.

"And I want to experience it all with you. I'm all yours, baby," she purred.

We stepped into the shower. Water drizzled on us as Sakura reached for the bath sponge and poured body wash all over it. Then she rubbed it gently on my naked body. She used her other hand to feel my body all over. I closed my eyes and moaned with pleasure.

When I opened my eyelids, she was kneeling, caressing my crotch. She rubbed my crotch using the sponge. I slowly knelt with her and kissed her moist lips as the shower sprayed warm water over us. Drizzling warm water. Then we stood up. I gently pushed her against the wall so that the front of her body was facing me. I gently ran my hand down her sexy waist until it reached her inner thighs. My fingers massaged her inner thigh and moved to her crotch where I pressed my fingers firmly. She moaned in pleasure and asked me, "Will you eat me out? Please? I've been fantasizing you eating me out." I whispered in her ear, "Anything you want baby. Let's make your fantasy a reality. Relax and enjoy."

I moved my lips from her ear to her cheek. I began kissing her body downward while my hands massaged her crotch. My lips moved from her cheek to her neck, to her breasts, to her stomach, and finally to her pubic area. I kissed and caressed with my mouth and licked her outer vagina. She moaned loudly, pleased. Using my hands, I gently separated her labia and licked her clitoris and her inner labia. She tasted sweet and tangy. Delicious. I could taste her all day. I continued to lick this area while she moaned. She said, "Yes. That's it. Keep at it. That feels so good, baby." Then I started to suck on her clitoris. Gently at first with increased added intensity while using my tongue to twirl and tap repeatedly. She arched her back and moaned loudly.

I sucked more of this area of her vagina while putting my face into a rocking motion. She placed her hand behind my head and beckoned me to keep going. At the same time, I glided my fingers along her vagina opening and massaged the entrance. I could feel her getting more wet.

As her clitoris grew stimulated and enlarged, I moved my mouth to her vagina opening and licked while using my pointer finger to massage her clitoris. My tongue entered her vagina in a twirling and tapping motion. She moaned and trembled as I did this. I kept at it feeling pleasure vicariously from pleasing her. I loved tasting her all over. She was sweet and tangy.

Suddenly, she grabbed my head and motioned me to stand up. I stood facing her. Her face was relaxed with a lot of euphoria, and large smile. She whispered in my ear, "I'm so turned on. I'm much more wet now. I absolutely loved the way you gave me oral sex. I was close to an orgasm just by you doing that. But I want you now to thrust me inside. Then for you to go back down and finish orally when I climax. I'm ready, baby." She took my dominant hand and licked my pointer and middle finger. She sucked on both fingers for added lubrication.

Smiling naughtily, my fingers crawled along her pubic area, tickling it. Sakura giggled and blushed at me. Her dark eyes and facial expression beckoned me to go further. She spread her legs widely and gently thrust towards me. I moved my fingers to her clitoris and firmly rotated clockwise while I kissed her neck. She breathed heavily, calling my name. I then inserted the two fingers inside of her vagina. Gently thrusting upwards.

"Ohhh yes." Sakura whispered. Her face became flushed and looked as if she were enjoying it. Her moaning became louder and increasingly erratic. She tilted her head and arched her back in pleasure. Then she began to hump against my fingers. I moved my fingers along with her body's rhythm. I could feel more of her wetness on my fingertips. I kissed her lips and caressed her breast with concentration on her areola and nipple.

"Mmm, that's good baby. You can go faster." She directed me. I increased the pace of finger thrusting along with intensity. She screamed in pleasure and trembled. "Yes, baby, yes! Harder." My arm started to ache, but I kept going. Harder. Faster. Stronger. Pounding. My fingers feeling her warm, tender, flexible and beautiful anatomy. I kissed and sucked on her nipple with the same gradual intensity. I felt her breathing very erratic, and suddenly the loudest moan I heard all night of her first orgasm. My fingertips detected a warm thick, gooey and tasty substance of her cum.

I broke the kiss from her breast and moved my mouth slowly down her slender, sexy body. Sakura stroked my head and continued moaning. I placed my hands on her waist as I kissed her pubic area. My girlfriend watched me quietly as I gently, but firmly licked her vagina. She spread her legs out wider. I opened the lips to its entrance and flicked my tongue crazily at her clitoris while lapping up cum. Super delicious. Sakura began to wiggle, trying to endure the overzealous amount of pleasure she was feeling. She placed her hands behind my head and made me press harder against her.

Soon I was banging my mouth on her. I could taste her sweet, warm juices on my tongue and lips. I pushed my face faster and harder each time I pounded her. It wasn't long until she reached her second climax and had a large orgasm. When I was done, I let the water from the shower faucet rinse my face of Sakura's secretions.

"Baby, you're so amazing. Tell me what you want and how you want it. I'll do it for you." Sakura whispered in my ear. I whispered to her something that I enjoyed receiving. She smiled at me and did just that.

Sakura turned me over to the wall. We both stood. My back facing her as her mouth ran down my back until it reached my bottom. She first caressed my buttocks before she slid her pointer finger into my asshole. A rush of goodness and excitement overcame me. Then she rubbed my clitoris and began sliding her fingers into my vagina in a similar way. I moaned in pleasure.

She did this for some time until I was close to climaxing. Then she turned me around and pleasured me orally. Her tongue went deep inside wiggling, going further and further. Soon her tongue was entering and existing like crazy and her fingers assisting. Oh, it felt so good. I had multiple orgasms and she was amazing at what she did.

We continued our love making with passionate kissing and numerous positions. We did it in shower and while in bed. Sakura and I took turns performing many maneuvers on each other, and it was spectacular. We listened to each other's requests and desires, which intensified the experience. We were connected the whole time. It was very intimate but also lots of fun. We even incorporated food – whip cream, cherries, and chocolate syrup. In addition to light kink, such as feathers and a blind fold. I could not imagine doing this with anyone else. Just her. It felt special. We made sweet love for many hours. I wanted it to last forever. It was paradise.

CHAPTER THIRTY-NINE

The heat. The sweat. The passion. The erotic motion. The bliss, pleasure and taste of fresh, unlimited, burning, sensational, exciting sexual intimacy. The feeling of sweet satisfaction and tiredness after performing complex, various movements and positions consisting of touching, feeling, tasting, and erratic breathing. What glorious delight! That's what sex was with your lover whom you share a deep connection.

I watched loads of love scenes in movies and television shows. I've read fantasies in stories. Reading or watching people make love was nothing compared to the real thing. It was a thousand times better. Sex was like being hypnotized or intoxicated with pleasure pills. The whole world becomes magnificent and all you can think about was how to satisfy you and the other person you're with. It was like ecstasy. It was a rush of adrenalin and excitement followed by relaxation and euphoria. It was something that you can't clearly grasp unless you've done it. I laid in bed with Jenna that night, naked and sweaty. The fan was on, but I still perspired. We cuddled, our warm, bare bodies against each other.

"I'm not a virgin." I thought. I repeated the sentence in my mind. The more I said it, the easier it was for me to believe it. I couldn't believe sex was so amazing. It happened all so fast, but every moment of it was incredible. And memorable. And precious. I could never ask for anything more out of a relationship when it came to sex.

"How was it? Are you satisfied? Did you enjoy it?" asked Jenna.

"Yes, love. Every bit of it. You were fabulous. It was a wonderful time that I will always look forward to with you. Was I any good?" She stared at me as if I was silly.

"Good? No, you were brilliant, darling." I blushed.

"Really?"

"Yes," she hissed. She tickled my ear with her tongue. I giggled.

"I love you." I whispered.

"I love you, too. Promise me that you won't fall for another woman as long I'm yours." I made a pledge to always remain loyal to her as she did the same for me. We kissed each other and before I knew it, we were making crazy, erotic love once again.

CHAPTER FORTY

Sakura and I took a stroll to the park. We sat on the swings and swung ourselves. The day was warm, sunny and a bit overcast at the same time. It was lovely.

"What do you know about vampires?" she asked me. I was surprised by her question.

"That was random." I said.

"I know, but I'm curious."

"Well, vampires are nocturnal, right? And they depend on the blood of other creatures. Of course, they prefer human blood than anything else since they are partially human, too. I guess you can describe them as being parasites."

"What if the nocturnal part is wrong? Can they walk in broad daylight, too? And what if that one thing about killing them with a dagger to the heart is a myth? What other weaknesses could they possibly have?"

"Why are you so curious about them suddenly? I thought you said they were ridiculous because they don't exist."

"I know, but I'm starting to believe in them." she said. I looked at her, awed.

"What caused this change?" I asked. She told me everything about her dreams and visions.

"Sakura, that's incredible. You can really foresee the future or past, and see dead people? I envy you. I've always been a fan of supernatural phenomenon," I said.

"I know. I wish I could trade with you." I laughed.

"Don't be silly. In fact, you should be grateful to possess such awesome insight and power."

"Do you really believe me?"

"Of course. I'm am a believer after all." She smiled.

"I'm glad you don't think I'm crazy."

"So, you still haven't figured out its weakness?"

"Nope. I hoped maybe you had an idea."

"I'm sure if it didn't eat or drink anything for a long time, it would eventually die of starvation."

"True, but I can't possibly prevent it from attacking. There are billions of people on this planet it can feed on. Plus, I bet it can feed off other animals, too. Not just people."

"Yes. That's the bitter drawback." I said. "I know I'm not much help, Sakura. I'm sorry."

"No, it's fine. At least you tried. I can't ask for nothing more out of you under these difficult circumstances."

"I wonder how it could be fond of you." I said curiously.

"No clue. And that alone sends shivers up my spine."

"Maybe…" I started.

"What?"

"Maybe it wants to mate with you?" I shrugged.

"Gross. No way. I won't let it. I'm in no mood to conceive a future Dracula." I laughed.

"Just a suggestion, my sweet cherry blossom." I said.

"Or maybe it wants me to be its heir. It might want me to take its place because perhaps its time is almost over. I do have powers to 'see' things so maybe that alone makes me a great choice. I would become a super vampire and I won't get caught."

"That's a valid possibility. You have no idea what gender it is?"

"No. I wish I knew."

"Me too." I said. I changed the subject. "What do you think of going to England over the weekend?"

"This weekend? We're doing this to visit your father, right?" she questioned.

"Yes, love. How did you know?" I smiled.

"I'm the one who's psychic," she whispered hoarsely and winked. I giggled.

"Well, are you interested?" She nodded and said that she would pay for her plane ticket. I insisted that I would cover her fare, but she stubbornly refused my offer. I gave in and finally agreed to her condition.

CHAPTER FORTY-ONE

I woke up in the middle of the night, sweating and gasping for air. Jenna was sound asleep beside me. I slowly removed her hand from my waist and walked to the dresser. I changed into my outdoor clothes and took a stroll. During the day, the neighborhood is always quiet and friendly. However, during the evening it's silent and eerie. I came prepared with a flashlight and pocketknife in my jacket pocket. I walked to the nearby park with intention of meeting the vampire. I dreamt of it waiting for me on a swing. It patiently waited for my arrival so that it could talk with me.

It was only a five-minute walk, but I strolled with heavy caution that it took me twice as long to get there. Just like in my dream, the person in the cloak waited for my arrival as the very swing I sat in earlier. It beckoned me to sit in the swing next to it, which Jenna occupied. I stood frozen, debating whether to take another step.

"Come on. I won't bite you. I need to talk with you." It had a voice of a woman and it sounded very familiar. I slowly walked to the other swing and sat down, never leaving my eyes off her.

"Listen. There's been a mistake. I'm not the one responsible for the killings." She looked at me with her yellow bright eyes from the dark cloak she wore.

"Who are you? And what do you want with me?" I asked. She removed her hood and exposed her face. It was Cindy Hendricks.

Cindy slowly took off her hooded black cloak and dropped it on the ground next to her. She wore nothing else but black, lacy undergarments. She stared at me with her bright yellow eyes. She looked sad.

"I'm sorry to trouble you, Sakura." She paused. "But I had no intention of hurting those people. In fact, I have no memory committing any crimes."

"What do you mean?"

"I mean, I guess I was the one that did it. But I wasn't aware of it. You know what I'm saying?"

"A little." I was stilled confused by her explanation.

"I mean, I felt like I was being controlled by something, or someone when it all happened. I'm not myself. This isn't me. I'm no vampire."

"That's creepy."

"Tell me about it. I just want to be normal again. I was never like this until that day when I snuck into Mr. Richard's house. I led him down to the basement, made them fall down the staircase unconscious, and sucked out the life of him."

"Do you have any idea who's doing this to you?" I asked.

"Someone with great psychic power. Someone who can control over peoples' minds and actions. I get the feeling that you know this person. And I'm not the only person that has done it. I didn't kill Robby Samson or that other woman in Australia."

"What? Who was she?"

"Her name was Lillian Baker. She was found dead with a pierced neck in a bathroom stall at a night club in Perth on Friday night."

I sat quietly where I had thoughts spinning in my mind. Jenna came into my mind. For a second, I had a feeling that maybe she was the one responsible for the crimes. Feeling stupid, I shunned that idea out of my head. I asked Cindy why her eyes were yellow. She said that she didn't know and that whatever's controlling her can also make her eye color change.

"Do you know who else could be controlled?"

"Frankly, anyone can. We are only human, and we can be easily impressionable to some extent. For all you know, you could be a 'vampire,' too." I shivered at that disturbing thought.

"I don't think I am. I haven't felt strange lately."

"You might not be aware of it. That's how I was at first, too."

"Maybe, but I refuse to believe it. I'm not that way." I said firmly.

"Anyway, the police tracked me down and they're very suspicious about me. They're convinced that I was the one responsible for Mr. Richard's murder because I was the last person they saw. I was their housemaid. I thought I'd stop by to let you know what's going on. Be careful, Sakura.

And be careful whom you trust. People can be deceiving." Cindy picked up her cloak and ran off in the distance, disappearing into the dark night.

I opened the front door and found Jenna in a red bathrobe standing in the living room next to the sofa. Her hands were folded. She looked utterly serious. She asked me where I was this late at night. I told her I couldn't sleep so I took a stroll to the park.

"And you didn't even bother to tell me?" she said angrily.

"I didn't want to wake you up." I said.

"You could have at least left a letter."

"I'm sorry. I didn't think of that."

"Obviously. You weren't thinking at all!" she yelled.

"Well, I'm sorry!" I said angrily.

"I was worried, Sakura. I was about to call the police, you know. So much danger is out there. I was going crazy over here hoping you would return safely in one piece." She turned around and faced the fireplace.

"I'm really sorry, Jenna. I didn't mean to worry you." I walked over and hugged her from behind. She broke my bind and sat on the sofa. I came over and sat next to her. She scooted over, leaving a big gap between us. I was feeling annoyed by then.

"Jenna, I really am sorry." I said sadly.

"You promised the last time that this kind of thing wouldn't happen again. Remember your trip to the doctor not so long ago?" she reminded me.

"I know. I feel awful about it. I really am. What can I do make it up to you?" I was desperate. I really felt guilty and I wanted us to make up soon. She didn't take her eyes off the empty fireplace. She told me she would think about it. She lied down on the sofa and looked as if she was going to sleep there. I asked her if she was coming to bed. She told me that she wanted to sleep in the living room for the night. I sadly walked upstairs and got into bed by myself.

CHAPTER FORTY-TWO

I woke up the next day to a sweet aroma smell in the kitchen. I walked over in my bathrobe and saw Sakura cooking breakfast. My hair was tangled and messy. Sakura was dressed in jeans and a white t-shirt. She greeted me good morning. I greeted her back, yawning. I asked her what she was making.

"My darling's favorite," said Sakura.

I walked over and looked in the pan. She was making me an omelet stuffed with cheese, red and green peppers, and shreds of carrots and celery. There was a wooden cutting board with variety of fruit. There were bananas, strawberries, peaches, apples, nectarines, grapes, and mangos. I asked her what the fruits were for. She said that she was going to make a healthy smoothie. She instructed me to go wash up and get ready for breakfast. I was about to protest, but I agreed since I knew she was doing all this to make up for last night. I took a shower upstairs and got dressed up in a pair of jeans and sweater.

When I got back, the dining table was set up neatly with plates, napkins, glasses, and silverware. We ate the food in silence and Sakura collected the dishes to wash them manually after we were done. I sat in the living room, quietly watching the news. Sakura came over and sat next to me after she was done washing the dishware. She turned the television off and stood in front of me.

"Hey, I was watching the tele." I said.

"I'm aware of that, but I have something to for you."

She ran to the kitchen and came back with a folded piece of paper and a red rose. She handed the rose to me and unfolded the paper.

"I stayed up last night writing a poem for you." She paused. "Well, I consider it more of a letter," I was surprised, but I stayed silent to listen to it. "It's titled my deepest apologies." She cleared her throat and continued: "My deepest apologies to you my love. I am sorry for bringing upon concern. I am sorry for fleeing without a word. My actions and thoughts were not considerate. When I saw how you reacted and most importantly how it made you feel when I returned, I knew I made a big mistake. Your disappointment had me in a trance of enlightenment. It made me realize how much you deeply care for me. I hope I have shown and proven much affection towards you like you have for me. You are my rose that I will forever water and take good care of. So, may you once more hear my sincere message and be convinced for I have made a mistake: My deepest apologies to you my love."

She handed me the paper. I folded it and placed it in my pocket. I walked to the dining room and placed the rose in the centerpiece. I took Sakura's hand and guided her back to the living room. I kissed her lips and held her close to me. I stroked her face and told her that the piece of writing was lovely. I forgave her.

CHAPTER FORTY-THREE

We left the house on Friday afternoon and took the plane to Sheffield. The flight wasn't very long. When we arrived there, it was raining and cold. Jenna and I wore matching outfits: navy blue jeans and sweaters that had the British flag designed in the front of it. Our feet were snuggly covered in white sneakers. We took our luggage and got into a taxi. She told the driver where to go. Before we left, she gave the driver money, which was British currency. I wasn't aware of how well prepared she came. The cab drove off.

I looked at her father's house. It was painted red and was two stories high. Jenna knocked on the wooden door. A tall, slender man in his early sixties dressed in a black sweater and black jeans opened the door and smiled. He had soft, green eyes and his hair was short and light brown. Strands of white hair were visible, but it wasn't too noticeable. His smile was very similar to Jenna's because two dimples formed. He spoke in a soft and soothing tone that was also like Jenna's.

"Welcome, mi ladies. Come. Come in, please." He had a thick, English accent.

"Hi daddy," said Jenna. She spoke with the same accent and kissed her father on the cheek. Mr. Watson escorted us to the living room. We placed our luggage in the guest bedroom.

"I hope you two don't mind sharing a room for a few nights," he said.

"We don't mind at all, daddy," said Jenna.

The three of us sat in the living room. The carpet was red, and the walls were beige. We each sat on a comfy, cushioned chair. A small low table was at the center of the room. Jenna's father went the kitchen and returned with a teapot. He poured some delicious, hot tea in each cup and served it to us. We thanked the kind man and sipped our drinks quietly. Mr. Watson was the first to speak.

"So, you're Sakura, correct?" he asked me. I nodded.

"It's delightful to meet you," he said kindly.

"The pleasure's all mine, Mr. Watson." I said.

"Please. Call me William. Mr. Watson is much too formal for me." He chuckled. Jenna smiled at me.

"So how was the wedding, Jen? And how's Elizabeth?"

"It was lovely, daddy. You should have been there. And mum's doing fine."

"That's good. I miss Lizzie." William turned to me. "That's what I call her mum, Lizzie or Liz." I nodded to indicate that I understood.

"Have you been taking good care of yourself, daddy?" asked Jenna.

"Yes, love. I have. Thank you for asking. Do you still work at that bank? What's it called again?"

"Washeendom Mutual. And I'm not working right now. I'm on vacation."

"Well, that's good, princess. Taking breaks are necessary."

"That's right, daddy. You should do the same."

"I am. Why do you think I have the weekend off this time? I want to spend time with you and your friend here." He winked at me. I blushed a little bit.

"Okay," said Jenna. The subject was dropped.

We spent the day looking through Jenna's and her father's photo albums. Most of the pictures were in black and white. I flipped through the pages and saw how much Jenna grew. She was such a cute baby.

"Jenna came out lovely." William told me. "The doctor said, 'this is a healthy one, yes. You should be proud.' She weighed eight pounds and eight ounces and little fluffs of hair stuck out of her head. It was quite a beautiful sight."

"I agree." I said.

There was a picture of Jenna on her father's shoulders at a park. She looked like she was five-years-old. Jenna pointed at it and said it was her favorite. I nodded my head. I looked through William's pictures growing up. He was a handsome looking fellow who had great charm. There were several photos with him and Jenna's mom. Elizabeth was stunning like her daughter. Like Jenna, she had long dark red hair and blue eyes. Her face was like Jenna's. Jenna had her pointed nose and soft lips. Jenna ended up inheriting her father's ears that perfectly suited her face and his smile and tone of voice. The three of us spent hours looking through the pictures until it was evening. William cooked us his homemade soup that was delicious along with fresh baguette and creamy butter.

Jenna and I slept in the bed at the guest room that night. It wasn't as spacious as the king sized one back at the house, but it was spacious enough for the two of us. I couldn't fall asleep. Jenna asked me what was wrong.

"Nothing." I whispered.

"It doesn't seem like it. You're quite quiet."

"I've just been thinking about my family."

"How are they?"

"I don't know."

"Oh."

"We're pretty distant." I said disappointedly.

"When did you last speak to them?"

"It's been years."

"Why is that?"

"They don't want to speak to me. Plus, I'm no longer wanted."

"What do you mean?"

"It's a long story." I said.

"I've got all night to listen," she said contentedly.

CHAPTER FORTY-FOUR

Sakura told me her hurtful childhood. It left me feeling depressed, but proud to know that she has gotten so far and didn't turn out bitter like her folks were to her. She grew up at three places: Manila, Tokyo, and Alicante. Her parents met in Spain when her mother, Salina Rizal was visiting Sakura's grandmother, Alberta Aloma in Alicante. Salina and Sakura's father, Kyo Hatsukawa met at a nightclub. It was love at first sight. They got married a month later and had Sakura in Tokyo.

The marriage didn't go too well because Salina didn't have a job and she wanted to go back to school for nursing. Kyo didn't like having a wife that was too educated or "smart for her own good" and he pressured Salina to stay as a housewife. Salina didn't like to be told what to do for the rest of her life, so she took Sakura and flew back to Manila to her family. Sakura's father got angry and soon there was a custody battle. The judge said it was best for the child to see both parents and declared that Sakura would alternate between countries every year to be with both. Her mother and father were not pleased with the verdict, but they bitterly accepted it.

Soon after the divorce, Salina found another man named Jose Lumana. Sakura never did like her mother's boyfriend because Jose was physically and emotionally abusive. She had many memories when Jose would come home intoxicated and beat her and her mother up when she lived with her mother. She would wake up the next day with numerous bruises and went through loads of physical and emotion pain. She even started cutting herself when she turned a teenager to feel better. She said that the cuts didn't hurt as much as they should have since she was feeling depressed.

Eventually, she became addicted to it to a point in which all she could think about when she got home from school was to lock herself in her bedroom and cut her thighs, arms, legs, and various parts of her body.

Sakura finally stopped when she almost died from accidentally stabbing herself in the stomach after trying to make a deep cut. She spent a week in the hospital and her mother became furious when she received a huge hospital bill. Until this day, her mother and boyfriend remained together.

Salina broke up with Jose after Sakura was hospitalized. Later she met and remarried a man named Theodore Mullen who was a nice, caring person to her mother and to her. This was when Sakura was in her late teens. She and Theodore got along well. He and her mother were happy together. Sakura felt happy for her mother and loved her mother very much. She felt close to her mother growing up.

Kyo found another woman, too. He was remarried. She was wealthy and prestigious because her father was the head of two oil companies. Her name was Hana Kawasaki. Sakura didn't like her because Hana despised Sakura from day one. Hana told her that she was going to steal her father from her for herself. She threatened someday to set her up for adoption. It never did happen, but she often reminded Sakura of it. Hana had a son from a previous marriage that ended in divorce. He and Sakura did not get along either and they were very distant. He and her siblings when their parents married and they each had no other siblings.

Sakura's repeated abuse from Jose made her very interested in martial arts. She received training from her father. By the time Sakura was twelve-years-old, she had mastered most fighting techniques with daily, rigorous practice and had vowed one day to defend herself and her mother. That day did not come because she was hospitalized, and her mother moved on from the relationship. After recovering from hospitalization Sakura went to Alicante when she was thirteen-years-old to live with her grandmother while her mother was busy with school to become a nurse and painter.

Alberta wasn't a good caregiver. She had a family secret of addiction to alcohol. She was good at keeping her secret from Sakura's mother. Alberta was also emotionally abusive to Sakura. Whenever she went out to go to a bar, she left Sakura with a male babysitter who sexually abused her several times. Sakura attempted many times to escape from mistreatment and almost defended herself using martial arts, but her abuser threatened her life. She was afraid and was reluctant to tell anyone for her safety.

Alberta eventually found out and fired him from babysitting. She called the police and he was arrested and convicted as a sex offender. She did not tell either of her parents of what happened. Sakura kept it a secret for years.

Another custody battle took forth between Salina and Kyo by the time Sakura turned fifteen. This time Kyo received full custody. Sakura could visit Alberta and Salina for a few days every year. Sakura grew closer to her father overtime, but Hana did everything she could to spend more time with him. Sakura often felt like she was second place in her priorities.

Sakura's decision to live in the US and study for medical school was unapproved by both Salina and Kyo. Alberta also disapproved, too. Salina said that being a doctor will burn her out and it's very hard. She said that you could get involved with crazy people and that the clients could get dangerous. Kyo claimed that being a medical doctor isn't a woman career. He wanted Sakura to take his place as a martial arts instructor so that his knowledge could be passed on to further generations. Alberta thought of the job as such a waste with so much schooling. She urged Sakura to become a nun and uphold the Catholic faith so that she and everyone in her family would enter heaven someday.

Sakura followed her heart and defiantly moved to Sea Town. She applied for several scholarships and got admitted for her exceptional grades and clean record. Sakura made some extra money by being a martial arts instructor. Ever since Sakura arrived to Washeendom when she was eighteen, she never spoke to her family. They seemed happier with her gone. Sakura became like a distant part of their lives. There wasn't much affection or fondness between them. Sakura felt better with firm boundaries between her and her family members at this point in life.

"Sakura, that's terrible. I've never been through anything like that before. I'm so sorry." I said. I kissed her cheek and gave her a hug.

"It's okay," she said. "You should be happy and grateful for having two loving parents who care for you and treat you right. I would have been lucky if I had at least one affectionate and supportive guardian. My mother was the closest to me growing up. So, I envy you for that. But I'm glad that you have good parents in the picture." She made great points. Plus, I was an only child throughout my life. I held her close to me under the sheets, cradling her body.

"I'll do everything I can to replace pastime bitterness and pain into affection, support, and pleasure." I whispered in her ear. Sakura gazed into my eyes.

"You're sweet, honey. But that's not very necessary. I appreciate your suggestion, though. I don't want to forget my past because it contributes to how I am today. Without the experiences I've obtained, I would be a different person. I probably wouldn't have gone to the US or have met you," she said.

"That's true, but the past can hurt." I told her.

"Yeah. But I see it two ways. You can either run and avoid the past. Or, you can confront, accept, and learn from the past. I tend to go for the second option." I smiled broadly.

"That's my smarty-pantsy cherry blossom." I said proudly. We rubbed noses and giggled. She asked me how my parents took the truth of my sexuality. I told her that they had no idea. It was also a secret.

"Seriously?" she asked, surprised.

"Yes. They don't need to know. Maybe they will one day. When we get married, that is." I winked at her. Sakura blushed and nodded.

"No one knows about it except you and Emi," she said. "It's hard to find people to trust. I had a difficulty with it growing up. That alone didn't give me the opportunity to make many friends. Emi was the only friend I had. I stayed at her house a lot in Japan when I lived with my father. My father didn't care, which was fine with me since I always had loads of fun at her place. It's quite depressing, actually." She frowned.

"Well, at least you had a close friend. I had lots of friends, but not any close friends, you know. I wasn't really close with anyone outside my family except with my numerous girlfriends, if you know what I mean." I winked twice. She giggled and hit my arm playfully. I yawned and we passionately kissed goodnight.

CHAPTER FORTY-FIVE

The rest of the weekend was a lot of fun. William took us out shopping and bought anything that we desired. I felt a bit guilty for picking out a lot of clothes. I liked the clothes they had in England. There was a wide variety and lots of the garments were extremely fashionable. I bought several dresses for various occasions from breakfast, to teatime and eveningwear. Jenna spent loads of money on makeup and beauty products. William even took some time to shop around for himself. He bought himself three dashing suits and a couple pair of new shoes. He seemed to have had a fun time with us.

I took loads of pictures of monuments and places throughout the country. I loved how classy and elegant the places where. Lots of areas had loads of history and Jenna did a fine job acting as a tour guide, addressing several time periods and facts. Her father pitched in to elaborate on the history. It was one of the most incredible times that I've ever had. Spending it with my darling and her father made the experience even better.

I received an unexpected call from my father on Sunday evening. Jenna, her father, and I were at a fancy restaurant in London. Embarrassed, I took my cell phone and continued talking in the women's washroom. My father usually spoke to me in Japanese. This time he spoke mostly in English.

"Hello? Father?" I said.

"Sakura-chan. O genki?" ("Sakura, how are you?")

"Genki desu. ("I'm fine.")

"Listen. I'm at the hospital now."

"Huh? What happened? Are you okay?"

"A little. I was shot."

"Oh my gosh! Who did it?"

"I don't know. But it's a woman.

"I'm sorry, Dad. I need to come see you. I'll be on my way."

"I won't make it. Tomorrow will be my last day. I'm calling to tell you this."

"What? Dad…"

"I've always loved you. And I have always been very proud. I've haven't always been a good father to you. And I am sorry. Please forgive me, Sakura."

Tears rolled down my eyes. I couldn't believe what I was hearing. My father never expressed any affection towards me. He always acted tough and serious around me. He always expected me to be strong and somber like he was. It was completely unexpected out of him.

"Thank you, Dad. I love you, too," I said tearfully. Then he hung up.

I washed my face to clean off my teary face. Jenna walked in. She asked me why I was crying. I told her the news. She frowned and held me, apologizing for what had happened. I told her it wasn't her fault and not to feel sorry. I felt guilty because my father's academy was going to shut down and be made as a new car shop for Hana. My father always wanted a son to take over for him. He had a son with Hana, but my half-brother, Toru was interested in the study of religion and supernatural phenomena more than anything else.

Jenna told me to take as much time as I needed to grief and feel my feelings and reminded me that she was there to support me in any way. I reluctantly agreed with her and returned to the table. I didn't say another word for the rest of the night.

We arrived back to William's house and packed our things. Jenna and I were leaving the next day at noon. Her father wouldn't be around to see us go because he had an operation to do early in the morning. Before we went to sleep, Jenna hugged and kissed her father goodnight. He went over and gave me a hug and said that he had a wonderful time getting to know me. I told him that he was very kind and was a great father. He became bashful by my compliment. He thanked me and hugged me again. Jenna seemed happy that the two of us got along well.

CHAPTER FORTY-SIX

We arrived back to Sea Town at two in the afternoon on Monday.

"It's weird how an eight-hour difference could be," Sakura commented.

"I agree. We just came back from the future. Get it?" I laughed at my lame joke.

"Haha," said Sakura.

We didn't bring much home with us. We only had our luggage and two bags filled with new clothes and souvenirs. Both of us walked upstairs, dragging our belongings to the bedroom. By the time we were done, we were exhausted. Sakura suggested that we go out for dinner. I thought that was a brilliant idea. I felt a little hungry. I went over to check the telephone in the living room to see what calls were made while we were gone. There was one message. I pressed the play button. A woman in a squeaky, mousy voice spoke.

"You aren't going to get away with what you've done. I'm coming for you." I knew it was Sally. Sakura and I looked at each other. She took out her cell phone and was about to dial 911, when the front door suddenly swung open with great force. Sally entered the room with a pistol in her hand, pointing the weapon at Sakura's head. My eyes widened, and I became fearful.

"I wouldn't do that if I were you," Sally told Sakura. Sakura placed her cell phone back in her pocket.

"Sally, don't—" I started.

"Just shut up, Watson. I don't want to hear from you!"

"Sally. Put the gun down." Sakura said calmly.

"Why should I?" Sally retorted.

"Because you would be in deeper shit if you don't." I said.

"I told you to shut up, Jenna," screamed Sally.

"You need help," said Sakura.

"No, I don't! Only I can help myself." Sally said bitterly.

"Yeah, right." I snorted sarcastically.

Sally pushed Sakura into me. We both faced our adversary. To our surprise, Sally closed her eyes and began breathing heavily. She licked her lips and sniffed the air. Her entire body vibrated, and she started to levitate off the ground. She growled and opened her eyes. Her eyes turned bright yellow. She bared her fangs and said in a hoarse voice, "Yes. I must kill the girl named Sakura. Yes, Master. I will not fail you like the others have done. I will not betray you, Master. I will not kill her with my predatory instincts, but with my weapon." She pointed the gun at Sakura. Without thinking of my own safety, I leapt in front of Sakura and took the shot. Blood gushed out of my right shoulder. I laid on the living room floor in pain, quietly groaning.

"Jenna!" screamed Sakura. She knelt and held my head. Tears rolled down her eyes. I smiled, happy that she wasn't hurt. I felt myself drifting off into another world. I fell asleep.

CHAPTER FORTY-SEVEN

I stood up and looked at Sally with a serious stare.

"You monster!" I yelled. Sally laughed loudly, pleased by what Jenna did.

"She deserved it." Just then, Sally disappeared like magic. It was very similar to how Lisa and Malto vanished. I knelt next to Jenna and told her to wake up.

"Jenna, please! Wake up. Don't leave me like this. I need you." I cried harder than ever on her wound. To my surprise, my tears seemed to be healing it. I continued to cry, hoping that the injury would fade completely. The blood moved back to the hole on her flesh until all was left was a bullet. I picked up the bullet and threw it in the garbage. I picked up Jenna and placed her on the sofa. I kissed her forehead and whispered in her ear to wake up. After a few minutes of unconsciousness, Jenna finally awoke. I embraced her tightly, extremely relieved that she was alive. She couldn't believe that she survived that shot.

"I could have sworn that I was a goner," she said, confused.

"I healed you with my tears." I said. Tears continued to run down my cheek. I was feeling very emotional. Jenna wiped my face and kissed me zealously. Jenna explained to me that when she was crossing over, something told her that it wasn't her time to die. It told her that she must stay with Sakura and keep her company. I looked at her warmly. Jenna smiled broadly at me.

"You know I wouldn't leave you, Sakura. I'm here to be with you the entire way." I grinned and told her that I was extremely glad that she was by my side.

"I owe you my life now, Jenna." I said.

"No. You shouldn't say that. I'm sure you would have done the same for me." I never felt happier until that very moment. I was starting to believe that it was fate that brought the two of us together.

CHAPTER FORTY-EIGHT

I rested on the sofa and closed my eyelids. Sakura just left to go on a leisurely bike ride. I had a reoccurring dream in which I was kidnapped by a cult whom I have encountered before in the past. They all wore black cloaks and followed orders of a person with great psychic abilities.

I witnessed their gathering at a dark cave in the woods within the Mountains. I couldn't see their leader, but he spoke articulately about how his human subjects were complete failures. At that moment, I opened my eyes, and found myself in a large, black garbage bag. My legs and arms were bind with rope and my mouth was sealed with duct tape. I struggled to get out of the sack, but something hit me hard on the head. I fell into a deep sleep.

CHAPTER FORTY-NINE

I arrived home an hour later to a silent house. The door was unlocked. I couldn't find Jenna anywhere. I called her cell phone and found out that she left it in the bedroom. Thinking that maybe she went to the store, I waited patiently for her to come home. Unfortunately, she didn't return that night. I got more worried and paranoid that I called the police. Two policewomen walked up the doorstep. They were the same officers Jenna and I spoke with at the station. The women recognized me.

"Hello, Miss Hatsukawa. We received a call saying that someone is missing," said the policewoman with blonde hair.

"Yes."

"Who?" asked the other older officer.

"It's my friend, Jenna Watson."

"How long has she been missing?" asked the blonde-haired officer.

"She's been missing for a few hours and I have no clue where she could be. She didn't leave anything when she left. Her car's still here and so were all of her belongings." The other officer questioned when the last time I spoke with her and I told them everything.

CHAPTER FIFTY

Someone spilled a bucket of ice, cold water on my face. I woke up in a dark cave. Candles surrounded the perimeter. I laid in the center of a gathering circle. I looked at the ground and noticed that it was engraved in a black skull image. Everyone wore the same clothing: black hooded cloaks. More frightening, all of them had bright yellow eyes. The crowd began chanting something that I couldn't recognize because it was in another language. It sounded like Latin. I wish I could understand them.

The crowd turned their heads to face the large center rock that was near the big gap in the gathering. I turned to see what they were looking at. Someone in a long, leather, navy blue hooded cloak levitated from the huge rock and stared at me. His eyes were not yellow. They were dark brown. He had an oval face with a light brown complexion. His hair was long, almost shoulder length and he had a scar on his left cheek. I predicted that he was young in his late teens. He opened his mouth and spoke to me in a deep, hoarse tone.

"Jenna Watson. It's good that you came," he said. Someone from the crowd took off the duct tape from my mouth.

"I came here against my will! I was abducted. That's a felony! Once the police —" I protested.

"Silence!" He bellowed. The entire word echoed through the cave. "You ran away from your duties. You fled and went into hiding from me. You have betrayed me, Jenna! You should be deeply ashamed of yourself!"

"I don't know what you're talking about! I don't know you! You've got the wrong person!" I said angrily. The young man chuckled sarcastically.

"You don't remember who you are, do you?" I stared at him extremely confused.

"Of course, I know who I am!" I snapped.

"Then explain," the man said calmly.

"I'm Jenna Watson. The daughter of William Watson and Elizabeth Smart. I grew up in England and Australia. I have a house in Sea Town, Washeendom. That is who I am!" I said this very quickly. The young man laughed genuinely. The others joined in.

"You forgot one important piece to your past, Jenna. It is your destiny. Never forget who you really are," the man said somberly. He stared at me gravely. My mind was completely blank.

"Who are you guys?" I asked timidly.

Everyone removed his or her hood. I was shocked to see who they were. I recognized three men and a young boy in the crowd. One was large and bulky-looking as a rock with long, frizzled green hair. I knew that was Fred Little from psychology class. The other was a slender, short man with a blue Mohawk. I knew he was Jack Johnson who was also in Mr. Richard's class. Another was a large man with a long, black, bushy beard and small spectacles. I remembered he was Jeff Romano from the Subpath restaurant. The teenage boy next to Jeff with long red hair and hazel eyes was Nick Truman. Sally Field was in the crowd, too. She had a sinister expression on her face. I knew there was something mysterious about her since day one.

Another woman stood in the crowd. She was tall, slim and had short, blonde hair with hazel eyes. I wondered who she was. The last person in the crowd caught my eye. It was my ex-girlfriend, Jessica Munson. My jaw dropped. I asked her what she was doing here. Jessica cleared her throat and looked at me seriously.

"I can't believe you erased your own memory of us, Jenna. I thought you would forever remember what we went through together," she said.

"What the hell are you talking about?" I yelled. "What is going on?"

"It is time!" they all said in unison.

"Jenna, it's time for you to be reunited with your own kind and to never flee again," said the young man in the navy-blue cloak. He floated over to me and placed his hand on my forehead. I felt as if I were electrocuted. My entire body from head to toe broke out in a huge, violent spasm. Within minutes, I remembered who I was. He handed me a cloak. I took my black hooded cloak and wore it with great pride. I anticipated in wearing Master's outfit someday. I was the future heir of among the small population of Immortal Beings - Vampires.

PART TWO

CHAPTER FIFTY-ONE

It's been a year since Jenna's mysterious disappearance. The investigation halted, and she was presumed dead. I couldn't believe such a thing if her body wasn't found. I believed that she was still alive somewhere. Jenna left a note in her will stating that I would inherit everything from her. I couldn't believe it. I now owned her house and her entire bank account, which consisted of millions of dollars. I wondered why she even worked if she could simply live a life without it.

My father's funeral took place not long after Jenna vanished. I flew to Tokyo to attend his memorial. Everyone from his family to friends and coworkers were there. I later found out that Hana mysteriously died with my father in the hospital room. Out of considerate sympathy for my father's desire to have wanted me follow, I attended her funeral, too. It took place the day after my father's. I was surprised that my half-brother, Toru did not show up to either memorial. Those few days in Japan were one of the most depressing days I've experienced.

I continued attending the University of Washeendom when it opened months later and taught myself how to drive Jenna's mustang. Every day I hoped that Jenna would walk up the doorstep and run into the house looking for me. I never saw Lisa or Malto again either. It was as if they never existed. I started to feel this way about Jenna, too. It felt as if the past year was a vague moment in time that was insignificant. I refused to believe that. Jenna told me that faith was needed through the fiercest adversity, and I knew she was right. I needed to believe in something. Jenna would have never intentionally left without saying a word to me. I was determined to find her kidnappers and make them regret ever taking the love of my life away from me.

CHAPTER FIFTY-TWO

I laid in bed with Jessica in my arms. She tickled my ear with her finger and licked my cheek.

"You must choose the next heir," she said.

"I know, but I'm not the leader yet."

"Your time will soon come, love. Choose me."

"Why?"

"Because I am worthy of it. I can be a great leader like you."

"Hmm." I shrugged.

"And that way I will always be near you, forever."

"I don't know. I have to be careful and wise when choosing the next leader."

"Come on. I'm the only member you know really well, and you know as well as I do that I'm totally qualified for the job."

I thought this over. Jessica wasn't the type I would choose to be a future leader of the immortal beings. She was too irresponsible and prioritized in excitement and risk taking more than anything. I couldn't trust her to take over such a high, honorary position. I didn't want to choose her, but I told her I would consider it. She kissed my lips and grinded her body against mine. She moved her hands on my body so sexily and seductively. I loved it. An urge to satisfy her and be satisfied quickly manifested. Soon we were making crazy, freaky love under the sheets.

That Thursday evening Master summoned my girlfriend and I to speak with him in person. I received his urgent message in my mind. He had the power to speak to other people through their minds. Jessica and I literally jumped through the rooftops of hundreds of houses to meet him in a cave at a nearby desert afar from town.

The weather was dry and humid, which was typical in Australia. I couldn't wait for the rendezvous to be over so that my girlfriend and I could return to her cozy, ventilated house. By the time we arrived at the cavern, the two of us were out of breath. I was dripping with sweat in my heavy cloak.

We entered the grotto where several lighted candles surrounded our Master. The other immortals, including Jessica and I didn't know his real name. Master was all we ever knew of him. We worshiped him because he was a fine, firm, strong leader who believed in our great purpose of obliterating those who have sinned on earth. Our mission was to track down people who have done horrid things and punish them for it. I felt very proud to take part in the operation. I was chosen to take over his position if he ever withers. Master said I was the most efficient and strongest immortal of all. Jessica and I slowly approached our leader who was sitting cross-legged on a large rock. We bowed our heads as a sign of respect and subordination. Then we sat down on the ground. The ground was covered with rubble.

"Welcome, my loyal Immortal Beings," he said. He lowered his head and slightly bobbed it. Jessica and I bowed our heads deeply, almost touching the ground.

"It is an honor to be in your company, Master." I said.

"Yes, it is, oh great one," said Jessica. Master smiled and began explaining what our next mission was.

Master sent an image of our subject with his psychic power. Julian Smith was a rapist who fled from his homeland in France to the Philippines. He raped over thirty female victims. Half of them were little girls. Smith was a thirty-two-year-old short man with dark brown complexion. He was masculine and strongly built for he was a former navy man. His eyes were green, and his hair was short, sleek and brown. He had a small, dark brown mustache that made him look a bit older. At the bottom of his chin was a small scar that he got during a physical outbreak with his crew when he was employed overseas. He had a tattoo of a Chinese character on his upper right arm. The character meant fierce bull.

"You two must stop this maniac before another woman gets hurt," said Master. The two of us bowed and solemnly promised to complete the task. Smith just arrived at Manila. His next crime will be done on Saturday.

His next victim will be a young woman who would be shortly visiting the country. He would sneak into her family's house at eleven o'clock, murder the victim's mother and kidnap the woman by force. The vehicle he would be driving is a black 1998 Honda Civic with a license plate saying, "Navy."

We got home late that evening and started packing our belongings.

"I can't believe he didn't inform us of this mission until the last bloody minute," muttered Jessica.

"It's a hassle. But those are our orders." I said.

"I'd rather stay here and spend time with you, Jenna."

"I know. I wish we didn't have to leave so soon." She turned around and asked me a serious question.

"Do you love me?"

"What?"

"I asked if you loved me."

"Sure, I like you, Jess."

"No Jen. I mean love."

"Love?" I said idiotically.

"Yes. Love. Not lust. There's a difference."

"True, but people get it mixed up all the time."

"You didn't answer my question."

I didn't feel like answering it because the truth was that I wasn't really in love with her. I was with her because I felt there was no one else out there to give a damn about me. It was quite depressing.

"Yes. I do." I said finally.

"No lie?" she asked.

"No." I lied.

"Good."

"Why did you ask?"

"Because I felt like I was being taken for granted."

"Don't worry. You aren't."

"Good." She kissed me and continued packing her items for the mission.

Jessica and I booked a flight to the Philippines after we packed. We would be leaving at two in the morning so that we would be at the city by late morning on the day of the crime. Both of us didn't get any sleep before the flight. However, we spent the flight snoozing.

CHAPTER FIFTY-THREE

I immediately packed my belongings in a large luggage bag when my mother called and told me that she needed help because Theodore was in jail. His fee to get released out of jail was one thousand American dollars. She needed that converted in pesos. I just arrived home from school when she called me. Theodore was falsely arrested for theft. I was shocked by the news that I told my mother not to worry because I would come soon to bail him out. I took a plane flight early Friday morning so that I could arrive at Manila by Saturday morning.

I arrived at the city jail and talked with my mom. Our conversation was in Tagalog. Theodore's clothes were filthy and torn for having stayed in jail for some time. It looked as if he hadn't washed in days. Like me, mom had her black hair long and straight. She was a very attractive woman with a slender body. She and I were about the same height and had similar faces. I looked at her as she hung her head low and her dark brown eyes were sad. Theodore looked sad, too.

I placed a hand on my mother's shoulder and told her that everything is going to be okay. I told her things will get better and suggested that I would stay with her if it was needed. Mom said that I shouldn't do such a thing and just go back to Sea Town. I told her that I couldn't just do that.

"Bakit?" she asked. ("Why?")

"Kase…" ("Because…") There was a long pause before I completed the sentence. I old her that she was my mother and that I wouldn't leave her or Theodore hanging like this. Tears came down her cheeks and she hugged me. Sobbing, she told me that she was sorry for not always being there for me when I was growing up. I said that it was okay and that there were no hard feelings. Mom wasn't convinced by my explanation. She really wanted to make it up to me and promised that she would someday. I told her it wasn't necessary, but said that if she wanted to, she could.

"Mahal kita, anak," said mom. ("I love you, my child.")

"Mahal kita nanai." ("I love you mom.")

After Theodore was released I took mom and him out to lunch. We sat at a round table outside of a seafood restaurant. I ordered pancit, which was a Filipino-style chow mien. Mom and Theodore ate fish sinigang with white rice. Sinigang was a Filipino dish consisting of fish broth, spinach, and tomatoes in a sweet broth. Theodore and mom thanked me for the lovely meal and for helping out with short notice.

The day was extremely humid and hot. It was the rainy season, but whenever it rained, it poured enough to create flooded roads. I reminisced swimming in the filthy water when I was little. I splashed at the jeepneys, which were mini Filipino buses that were brightly decorated and labeled after saints.

Across from where we sat was a suspicious looking man with sunglasses. I glanced at him through the corner of my eye and saw that he was closely observing me. The stranger was short and masculine. He had a dark brown complexion. His hair was short, sleek and brown. He had a small, dark brown mustache. He wore a tight white t-shirt and brown cargo pants. I tried my best to ignore him so that I could enjoy the time I spent with mom and Theodore.

CHAPTER FIFTY-FOUR

Jessica and I arrived at Manila with one thing on our minds: food. We slept the entire flight and hadn't eaten anything for nearly a day. We stayed a small hotel room that had a lovely view of the city through the large windows in the living room. It was my first time going to Manila and I found it quite noisy, busy, and heavily congested. The pollution and poverty were terrible, and I yearned for some fresh air elsewhere. After we got our items situated and organized we walked to the nearest restaurant. Jessica offered to buy the food as I found seats for the two of us. I sat alone for a few minutes at a small, white table, enjoying the sunshine.

Three tables away from me was the criminal, Julian Smith. I closely watched him and noticed that he was staring at someone across from him. The woman had her back to me. She was accompanied by another lady who appeared older than she was and an older gentleman. I assumed the women were the next victims.

The young woman stood up and walked inside the restaurant to get napkins because she spilled her glass of water. She wore a flowery, pink, skirt that reached down to her knees with a matching white tank top. Her hair was long, thick, and black with bangs that covered her forehead. I peered at her face as she walked passed me and noticed she had a small, cute nose that suited her lovely oval face. Her eyes were dark brown. I had a strange feeling that I knew her, but I didn't have any memory of it. I had an urge to leave my seat and introduce myself, or possibly get her phone number or email address so that I could get to know her more and stay in touch. However, I knew that I wasn't here to fool around, or make friends. I remained where I was and kept an eye on Smith.

Jessica returned with two bowls of pancit. I asked her if there was any meat in mine. She assured me that there wasn't a single piece of meat and she remembered I was vegetarian. I informed her Smith was nearby and she became much more alert and cautious.

As the women were leaving, Smith stood up and started following them. He got into his vehicle and followed the ladies and then gentlemen in a jeepney. My partner and I called a taxi and we followed Smith. He led us to the women's house. It was a three-story green building where tenants in numerous rooms for rent occupied the entire third floor. The two of us hid behind a tree and watched as the two women and man entered the building. Smith looked through a pair of binoculars and observed the ladies. When the door closed, Smith drove off. I didn't think he noticed us following him to where he was staying in a small building across a small pet store.

Jessica and I spent the rest of the day at the pet store hanging around. We waited for sundown. Many customers bought birds, cats, and dogs for pets. Looking at the dogs reminded me of my Dalmatian, Sammy when I was a child. He was so cute and active. We spent a lot of time together. When he passed away on my tenth birthday, I never wanted another pet because I didn't think any other animal could ever replace him. When it was ten-thirty at night, Jessica and I carefully watched the green building from the rooftop of the pet store because Smith was making his way back to that house.

CHAPTER FIFTY-FIVE

Mom and I had a long discussion about how things have been for the two of us for the past few years of not seeing each other. Her relationship with Theodore was going well overall. She recently finished her schooling to be a nurse and started working at a nearby hospital. On her spare time, she liked to paint, and she did good work. She sold a few of her works but claimed no one seemed to notice her great talent. I agreed with her and supported her talent wholeheartedly. Mom was a spectacular artist. I admired her for it because it was always so accurate and precise. I wasn't artistic at all and I sometimes wished that I inherited something like that from her.

She asked me how life was coming along for me and I told her I was doing okay. I was still teaching martial arts at the University and I was still taking the courses that were needed to fulfill my future career in medicine. I didn't tell her about Jenna or the killings that occurred in the area. Even after a year, the police found no trails that would lead them to the people responsible for the crimes. A few more deaths that were similar took place in other parts of the country. The incidences spread not only nationwide, but globally. The news was calling the reoccurring events as a worldwide crisis that had be stopped. I had a feeling that no matter how much investigation the government or police endeavored, they wouldn't be able to stop it. The situation was much too complex and widespread to unravel the mystery.

Before mom went to bed, she asked me how my father was doing. I was astonished that she wasn't ever notified of his death a year ago. She cried so hard about it. I comforted her as much as I could, saying that he didn't die in vain. She felt terrible because she didn't show up to his funeral. I told her not feel awful because she wasn't the only person who didn't attend. She asked me who else couldn't show up and I told her that Toru was absent for both father's and his own mother's memorial. Mom seemed disappointed to hear the news. She hugged me and made me promise to come to her funeral when that time came. I promised that I would. I helped her to her bed and kissed her goodnight. Theodore as already fast asleep.

I walked out of her bedroom and sat at the kitchen table. I felt thirsty, so I opened up the refrigerator to get a glass of water. As I closed the door and started walking backwards, I bumped into someone. My back was faced at the person, so I turned to around to see who it was. It was the creep that appeared to be stalking me back at the restaurant. He had a knife in his hand.

I started to run, but he tugged on my hair and sealed my mouth with is hand. He placed the knife on my throat and whispered in my ear to remain silent or he would slice it off. I knew how to escape in the position I was in, but it was too risky. I didn't want to get hurt.

Just then, a person in a black hooded cloak appeared in front of us. They stared sternly at the intruder. The person said to the man in a hoarse voice to leave, but the man refused. His arm and leg began to tremble, which made me thought that he was scared. The figure in black glowered at him with their bright yellow eyes and started floating above us.

The man got scared and started running away. The hovering figure stopped him before he could reach the door. The figure pinned him to the ground and looked as if it were devouring his neck. I watched in fear as they sucked the life out of the man. I was about to turn around and flee when another person in a black cloak appeared behind me and sealed my mouth with their hand.

Startled and bewildered, I struggled to escape, but the figure told me to remain calm and everything would be over soon. The person had a female voice. It spoke gently and softly. She sounded very familiar. I sniffed her hand and realized it smelled like lavender. For a moment, I thought it was Jenna, but it seemed impossible that she could be involved in such a situation. Once the other figure finished feeding on the intruder's blood, they stood up and beckoned the other to come over.

"Go ahead. I'll catch up," she said.

"Are you sure?" her partner asked. I noticed the other voice was female.

"Yes," the other said. Her partner nodded and faded in thin air. Aware that she wasn't armed, I rammed my elbow into her gut, hard. She winced and fell to the floor. I turned her over on her back and removed her hood: It was Jenna.

CHAPTER FIFTY-SIX

I pretended to be knocked out as the young woman looked at me, shocked. I quickly stood up and pinned her to the floor. My hands were wrapped around her throat and I started to choke her. Master was commanding me to kill her through strangulation. I felt out of control. It was as if my hands and fingers weren't connected to my body and they belonged to someone else. I had no intention of hurting her, but I couldn't help it. I looked at her as she struggled for air. She tilted her head and tried to speak.

"Jenna…it's me…" she said through erratic breaths.

"*What the bloody hell am I doing?!*" I asked myself. I wanted to stop right at that moment, but Master urged me to resume the task.

"*VERY GOOD, JENNA. NOW CONTINUE WITH THE JOB. STRANGLE HER GOOD. YOU HAVE EXCEPTIONAL FORM AND ACCURACY,*" said Master.

My grip tightened, and I pressed harder on her throat. Suddenly, she fell unconscious. I removed my hands from her neck and stared at my palms. Tears of anger dripped from my eyes.

"*Oh shitty! What have I done?!*" I thought. I felt utterly miserable and angry.

"*WELL DONE, JENNA,*" praised Master.

"But why her?" I yelled out loud.

"*SHE'S DANGEROUS.*"

"That's not true. We were sent out to save her."

"*WRONG. SHE'S HARMFUL, JENNA.*"

"She was innocent!"

"*NO, SHE WASN'T.*"

"*How the bloody hell is that?!*" I asked with my mind.

"*SHE WAS A THREAT TO US ALL. ESPECIALLY TO YOU.*"

"As if!" I thought snobbishly.

"SHE HAS A TERRIBLE POWER TO FORESEE THE FUTURE AND PAST. HER VISIONS COULD UNRAVEL OUR SECRETS AND PUT US ALL IN GRAVE DANGER. WE MUST DO EVERYTHING WE POSSIBLY CAN TO ASSURE THE SAFETY OF OUR KIND. THIS YOUNG WOMAN IS NOTHING BUT SOMEONE WHO CAN'T BE TRUSTED. SHE MUST BE DESTROYED QUICKLY!"

"No! She didn't do anything wrong! Our sole purpose is to only punish those who have sinned. You're wrong!!!"

"NOW LET'S NOT GET CARRIED AWAY AGAIN. I AM THE MASTER, NOT YOU. EVERYTHING I SAY IS TRUTH AND EVERYTHING I DO IS RIGHT. UNDERSTAND?"

"But what about virtues and ethics?

"WHAT ABOUT THEM?"

"Should we consider what is right and wrong here? I really believe I have done a crime to this lady. I have taken away an innocent life. I cannot live with this."

"REMEMBER, I AM YOUR LEADER. AND I ASSURE YOU THAT YOU ARE DOING NOTHING WRONG. EVERYTHING YOU HAVE DONE UP TO NOW HAS BEEN THE RIGHT THING. DON'T WORRY OR QUESTION IT NOW."

"I don't want this anymore. I cannot live like this. I wish I wasn't an Immortal Being."

"YOU MUST BE PROUD TO BE IMMORTAL. YOU LIVE FOREVER. YOU STAY YOUNG AND ATTRACTIVE. YOU NEVER DIE, JENNA. WHAT A WONDERFUL GIFT TO HAVE, DON'T YOU THINK? IF ONLY EVERYONE COULD LIVE FOREVER. YOU GET TO WITNESS GREAT CHANGE IN THE WORLD AND YOU WILL LIVE THROUGH ALL PARTS OF HISTORY. IT'S WHAT MANY HUMANS CRAVE FOR. POWER. ENTERNAL LIFE AND NEVER EXPERIENCING DEATH."

"I'd rather live one life and experience it all, and die in peace than to live forever and watch all my loved ones die, and for me to be miserable!"

"NO NEED TO WORRY, JENNA. ALL YOUR LOVED ONES ARE IMMORTALS. EVERYONE WHO HAS SIGNIFICANCE WILL LIVE FOREVER WITH YOU."

"*I could care less about them. They aren't my friends. They don't truly respect me. Sally hates my guts and Jessica is using me for status gain. I don't consider them as loved ones.*"

"*THEN WHO?*"

"*My parents who raised me in this life and…*"

"*AND?*"

"*Whoever this person is in front of me.*"

"*BLAH! FORGET ABOUT HER. YOU DON'T EVEN KNOW HER.*"

"*I don't believe you. I know in my heart that I know her!*"

"*HA! THAT'S RIDICULOUS.*"

"*Go away! Get out of my head!!!*"

"*I'M AFRAID THAT ISN'T POSSIBLE. I HAVE THE RIGHT AND THE POWER TO CONTROL YOU AND YOUR MIND, ALONG WITH THE OTHERS. YOUR MEMORIES ARE ALSO REGULATED THROUGH ME, JENNA. IT IS YOUR DESTINY TO TAKE OVER MY PLACE. I DON'T WANT YOU EVER LEAVING!*"

"*Fuck you!*"

"*NOW FINISH THE TASK! DRINK HER BLOOD WHILE SHE'S STILL UNCONSCIOUS. NOW!!!*"

"*No! I won't!*"

"*DO IT RIGHT NOW, JENNA!*"

"*No! I want nothing to do with this! Stay out of my life!*"

"*YOU CAN NEVER ESCAPE ME, JENNA.*"

I stood up and covered my ears. The young woman woke up and looked at me.

"Jenna? Is that really you?" she said. I looked at her confused.

"How do you know me?" I asked.

"Jenna, It's me. Sakura," she said.

"Sakura?" I repeated. The name sounded vaguely familiar. I scratched my head. Sakura sat up and held my hand. I pulled it away as if her hand was diseased. She looked hurt and sad.

"Don't you remember me, Jenna? I can't believe you've forgotten me."

"What's to forget?" I asked. Tears rolled down her cheeks. I suddenly felt guilty for some reason.

"*SHE KNOWS YOU BECAUSE SHE'S PSYCHIC, JENNA. SHE'S ONLY USING YOU SO THAT YOU WOULD DISOBEY ME AND*"

MAKE YOU QUIT YOUR DUTY TOWARDS YOUR KIND. DON'T LET THIS PATHETIC HUMAN TAKE ADVANTAGE OF YOU. SHE'S COMPLETELY VULNERABLE. SHE WOULDN'T DARE HURT YOU. NOW'S YOUR CHANCE. FINISH HER!"

"No. She knows me, and I used to know her until you erased my memories of her, huh."

"IT WAS FOR YOUR OWN GOOD. NOW FINISH THE DAMN JOB, YOU PROCRASTINATOR!"

"No!" I screamed and closed my eyes. "Go away! Get out of my head!"

"Jenna, what's wrong?" asked Sakura. She looked very worried and I was feeling more terrible by the minute.

"What's wrong?" I repeated to her. "I'll tell you what's wrong. It's my damn head. He won't fuck off!" Sakura winced and trembled.

"W-Who is doing this to you, Jenna? What's happening to you?" she stuttered in great concern.

"TIME IS TICKING, JENNA. DO WHAT'S RIGHT AND GET THE TASK DONE RIGHT NOW!"

"Quick, where's a mirror? And hand me a knife. It doesn't have to be a big one." I said. I took off my cloak and threw it on the floor.

"Why?" she asked.

"Just do it!" I yelled.

Sakura ran to the kitchen and handed me a small cutting knife. She guided me to the bathroom. She watched me as I looked at myself in the mirror. My face looked clean and my flesh radiated and felt smooth. I loved my face and I was going to regret making a mark on my forehead.

"WHAT ARE YOU DOING?" asked Master.

"I'm doing what I've done before. I'm going to get you out of my head. It is I who will control my mind. My feelings and thoughts from now on. Not some pathetic, desperate jerk like you! Now get out!!!"

"NO!!! STOP IT!! DON'T DO SUCH A FOOLISH THING!"

"Bite me! You asshole."

I closed my eyes as I dug the knife in my forehead, creating a small, straight, vertical line. I stopped before it reached the top of my nose, moved the knife to the center of my head and dug it in my flesh, making a straight, horizontal line. Then I slowly opened my eyes. It looked as if there was a cross on my head.

"Please. To the Universe. Forgive me for what I have done and caused to this woman" I said. I placed my hands together as if I was praying.

"SHUT UP!" squealed Master.

"Forgive me for straying off into the darkness. Bless all who love thou and forgive all who have done wrong in this world. Help me overcome this darkness within me. Guide me back to light and back to the goodness of the Universe."

"NO!!" screamed Master. *"YOU...WON'T...GET...AWAY..."* His loud voice grew fainter and fainter. I sighed in relief when I could no longer hear his voice anymore and therefore, can no longer access my mind or my memories. My memories with Sakura returned. My life was back into my own hands."

CHAPTER FIFTY-SEVEN

I watched in fear as Jenna cut her forehead and started to pray. I couldn't comprehend why she was acting so bizarre, but I didn't intervene. Every moment seemed crucial and it was a bit intriguing to witness it all. After she was done, she asked me for a glass of water so that her mind would clear up.

I handed her a glass of iced water and watched as she slowly drank. She looked the same when I last saw her, except she seemed to have grown an inch. She handed the empty cup to me and said thank you. She wiped her mouth with her hand and I guided her to the living room. We sat on the couch and started talking. I looked at her face and realized that the cross on her forehead was already healing very quickly. I pointed at it and asked how it could be possible.

"It's because I'm Immortal. Whenever I'm wounded, I heal fast," she explained.

"So, my tears never cured your gunshot wound." I said.

"That's right. It didn't."

"Why didn't you recognize me? You acted as if I was a total stranger." My heart sank when it happened.

"I'm very sorry, Sakura. Master erased any memory of you when I was kidnapped a year ago."

"What happened? And who's Master?" I asked. She explained everything to me. I listened attentively, never leaving my eyes from her gorgeous face. I noticed that she started to blush a little bit. Maybe I was making her feel uncomfortable. I took her hand and held it gently.

"I'm so happy that you're alive," I said.

"What? Didn't you listen to me?" she asked.

"Sure, I did. And it must be tough to be in a spot where you are. Having to carry the burden of high expectations among your kind and being dictated by someone you don't like."

"But, aren't you ashamed of what I am? I wasn't the woman whom you thought I was. I lied to you. I'm not normal, Sakura. I'm an heir of a something very dark and I can do wrong and harm. I'm not even human," she said in a disappointing manner. I stroked her hand placidly.

"So?" I replied indifferently. "Just because you're different doesn't mean that I don't like you or that I don't accept you. I love you just as much as before. Probably even more. I fell in love with Jenna Watson. I love every part of you, regardless of what you say negatively about yourself. I don't care what you are. You're the woman who carried my heart and saved my life. I still love you very much." I leaned forward and kissed her lips. I wiped a small stream of tears off her cheek.

"T-Thank you," she whispered in my ear and hugged me tightly. "Thank you for loving me and accepting me for who I am."

CHAPTER FIFTY-EIGHT

"Listen, Sakura. I must leave. The other Immortal Beings are going to search for me. It was lovely to see you again." I kissed her forehead and stood up. Sakura grabbed my wrist.

"I'm not going to let you go alone," she said firmly.

"No. You stay here. It's a lot safer."

"Maybe so. But I'm not going to let you leave me a second time. I don't want to lose you again, Jenna. Please. Let me come along."

"Sakura, I'm not letting you come and be with me. You're bound to get hurt because it's dangerous. It's unacceptable and I cannot let that ever happen to you."

"Come on, Jenna. A struggle alone isn't worth it. It's better if you have the right company."

"You're wrong. This doesn't involve you, Sakura. I must battle this on my own. That way no one else I care about will ever get hurt."

"Jenna, it's my life and I get to decide where to go and who to be with. I want to be with you. Don't you want to me to?"

"Of course, I do, silly. It's just very risky."

"Sometimes risk-taking is necessary when doing the right thing. No matter what you say, I'm going with you."

I looked at her sternly. I felt so angry at that moment. However, I couldn't help but reluctantly allow her to come along. Deep in my heart, I loved her company and facing the world together was what I preferred. I would do anything to keep her safe.

We flew back to Sea Town the next day, and I got reunited with my belongings and house that I left for Sakura. I couldn't believe that for an entire year I never once thought about Sea Town, or how cozy my aunt's house was. I missed it very much, especially my red mustang. It surprised me that Sakura knew how to drive, and she was extremely skilled at it. She didn't need my lessons because she picked it up on her own.

We drove to Downtown to a salon shop so that we could have new looks. I was content with the way I looked, but to successfully go under hiding, I knew that I had to change my entire identity, including my physical features. I refused to have my hair cut. Instead, I agreed to change my hair color to black. I wore green eye contacts and used a black sharpie to draw a mole next to my nose. Sakura had her hair layered and cut to shoulder length. She dyed her hair golden brown and wore hazel colored eye contacts. She looked great in her new look. I could hardly recognize her. She told the same thing to me when she saw me after the makeover.

We came back home and cooked dinner. I looked through the refrigerator to see what I could make. I found a package of tofu, chopped vegetables, and string of noodles.

"Do you mind if I make a tofu pasta?" I asked Sakura. She was sitting on the porch.

"I don't mind. I'll eat anything," she said. "Do you want any help?"

"No thank you. I'll be fine."

We ate our meal in silence for the first few minutes. I took a sip of red wine and resumed eating from my dish.

"Do you think they'll find us?" asked Sakura.

"I don't know." I said.

"How long were you hiding before?"

"Ever since I inherited this house."

"Wow. That long?"

"I suppose."

"I bet this is the first place they're going to check out when they come looking for you."

"You're right. But they wouldn't recognize me. Just tell them I'm a friend of yours from some other state and I'm just visiting." She nodded, and we continued our meal in silence.

After we ate, the doorbell rang. Sakura answered it. The person was a tall woman with short blonde hair and hazel eyes. She wore a brown fur coat and jeans. It was Cindy Hendricks.

"Cin—I mean, how can I help you, miss?" asked Sakura. It sounded as if Sakura already knew her.

"I'm looking for Jenna Watson. Have you seen her?" asked Cindy.

"I'm sorry. But she disappeared a year ago and she has not been found," said Sakura.

Cindy peered inside and saw me walking in the living room. She asked if she could come in. Sakura welcomed her inside and closed the door. The three of us sat at the dining room table. Sakura and I sat next to each other as Cindy situated herself across from us.

"You two don't need to hide," she said solemnly. "I'm on your side."

"What do you mean?" I asked. I was getting nervous.

"Don't be stupid. I know it's you, Jenna. And Sakura, you look swell today." My jaw dropped.

"How did you know it was us?" asked Sakura.

"I've seen enough of you two to know when you're undercover. The others don't know where you are and are frantically searching for you. You can't stay here for long, though. I'll tell them that I didn't find you here. I would advise you to leave town by tomorrow morning. It's not safe here," she warned.

"Why should we trust you?" speculated Sakura. "You do work for him, don't you?"

"Yes. I do. So, does she!" Cindy pointed a finger at me and looked at me seriously.

"I don't want any part of it anymore. I quit." I said.

"You can't run from what you are, Jenna," said Cindy.

"But she can change who she is as a person. She doesn't have to accept her promotion. She has control over her own destiny," argued Sakura.

"Wrong! She was chosen since birth. And the rest of us were born subordinate and were assigned to watch over her. She can't escape it."

"I said I don't want any part of this!" I yelled. I was shocked by how I couldn't control my temper. I calmed down as Sakura caressed my back.

"I don't care what you want, Watson. I'm only helping you get away because I feel like it's the right thing to do. Even if it means acting defiantly and betraying Master. And I'm also doing it for her." She pointed at Sakura.

"What?" I said.

"You're lucky to have someone as special as Sakura, Jenna. I want you to take good care of her for me," said Cindy. Sakura blushed.

"How do you even know her?" I asked suspiciously.

"Jenna, it's okay. Cindy gave me a ride home after the shopping experience at that Safepath in Evernette." Sakura explained.

"That's right," said Cindy. I got jealous, but I knew that Cindy meant well by what she said about Sakura. I thanked her and agreed that my girlfriend was indeed special and that I was a lucky gal. Cindy stood up and was about to leave.

"You stay out of trouble now, lass," she said to Sakura. She turned to me. "I'll tell Master that you're too clever for your own good." I thanked her and escorted her out the front door.

I shut the door behind me and faced Sakura in the living room.

"We can't run away forever," she said.

"I know." I admitted.

"You're going to have to face this guy and conquer him."

"I can't."

"Why?"

"I'm weak."

"No, you aren't."

"Yes I am. I'm merely a subject. A servant. I'm dirt."

"That's not true."

"Yes, it is." I insisted.

"I'm sure he wouldn't have chosen you to be his heir if you were a weakling."

"I know, but I don't know his weakness. He doesn't seem to have any. He's much too divine and powerful. I can't compete with his psychic ability."

"Yes, you can, Jenna. You're strong and I know you will do fine."

"I don't know." I was doubtful.

"Where's his headquarters?" she asked.

"In Japan. Tokyo to be precise. It's at a temple on the outskirts of town."

"Then let's go there and beat him at his own game," she said enthusiastically.

"I don't think so, Sakura. There are too many guards and I don't know what his weakness is."

"I'm sure after a few trial and errors, we'll figure out his weak spot."

"I wouldn't be too optimistic if I were you. And what are you saying 'we' for? I'm doing this alone."

"No way."

"Yes way."

"Remember what Cindy said? She told you to take care of me."

"And that's what I'm doing. I'm taking good care of you if you stay here. It's safer."

"That's wrong and you know it. He wanted me dead. So, if you leave me, you're giving me a death penalty."

"If I leave you, there would be no chance of him ever harming you because he wanted me to hurt you. He wouldn't have had someone else do it."

"Why not?"

"Because that's just how his mind works. He chooses specific Immortal Beings to execute certain people." I explained.

"I'll cry if you leave me here," she wined.

"That doesn't work with me." I said firmly.

Sakura started to whimper hurtfully. I got agitated and stomped my foot. I really didn't want her to win another argument. Not over this matter.

"Jenna. Let's face this beast together. If I was a threat, then I'm sure I have something that he's afraid of. I still have visions, and I'm sure I can be a big help." She frowned. I felt guilty for rejecting her help.

"Fine." I muttered.

"What?" she asked.

"I said fine." I repeated loudly. She smiled, jumped energetically, and gave me a massive hug.

CHAPTER FIFTY-NINE

We followed Cindy's advice and left the house soon after Jenna agreed to take me along. I drove us to Emi's cabin in the Mountains. When Emi left to go back to work this year, she handed me a duplicate key. I asked her why she gave me the key.

"If you ever need to get away from the noisy city, you are always welcome to come and stay here. There won't be much to eat, so bring some food in advance," said Emi.

"Thanks, Emi. You're an amazing friend," I said.

Jenna turned on the radio as I drove on the highway. We listened to the meteorologist, Renee from Pacific Northwest Highlighting News.

"Good evening everyone. I'm your weather woman of the evening, Renee. Tonight, is going to rain hard. Expect to see rainfall throughout the state from both sides of the Mountains. It was a gorgeous, sunny, warm day today so hopefully all of you got to enjoy that while it lasted. The temperature was nearly seventy degrees, which is unusual for this time of year. Tomorrow however, will be a lot cooler. Expect temperatures to be in the fifties. Tomorrow is also Halloween. It looks as if the evening is going to be clear and dry when the pouring stops until nightfall. Remember to wear warm costumes and bring those flashlights. Here's a prediction of the how following week will look like —" Jenna turned off the radio.

Jenna dug through her purse and pulled out a book. She flipped through the pages searching for something.

"What book is that?" I asked. The book was small and green.

"It's a book on astrology."

"Where did you get it?"

"I had it since I was a kid. It's pretty old." She was right. The front cover was torn and so was the back.

"Hmm. Is this book about horoscopes?"

"Yes. In fact, it says here on the cover: A horoscope guide for everyone."

"What sign are you?" I asked.

"I'm Taurus. What about you?"

"Pisces."

"Interesting. When's your birthday? I'll read you your horoscope."

"I don't believe in them."

"I knew you were going to say that. They're still fun to read."

"Fine." I told her my birthday.

"Okay." Jenna flipped through the pages. "Here we are. It seems like you have two passages. It says here your mystical gem is an aquamarine stone. Your fortunate day is Saturday. Your fortunate numbers are three and seven. Your lucky colors are aqua and green."

"Let's hear the passages." I suggested.

Jenna cleared her throat and continued reading, "You were born Pisces with Aries tendencies. This is because you were born at the cusp. You are intelligent. You are creative. You are a quick learner and a skilled observer. The planets you rule are Neptune and Mars. You can achieve great things. You are trusting and considered a safe person in the eyes of others. You are a big traveler."

"Wow. Very interesting." I said.

"Wait. There's another passage," Jenna explained. "It says here you are romantic. You are thoughtful. You tend to be attracted to people older than you. You can only be with one person at a time emotionally and physically. Once you are with someone you are loyal, loving, and giving. You enjoy expressing your love and commitment. You are playful and an attentive companion. You make a great romantic partner and a lifetime friend."

"What do you think? Does that sound like me?" I asked.

"Yes, there is resemblance. You do like to hang around people older than yourself." She winked. I laughed. I asked her to read her horoscope, so we could compare.

"Okay," she agreed. "It says here that my mystical gems are emerald stone, diamond, and coral. My fortunate day is Friday. My fortunate numbers are five and six. My lucky colors are pink and white. I have two passages as well. The first passage says my ruling planet is Venus. I am intelligent. I am charming. I have a huge capacity to be affectionate and loyal to people who are close to me. I tend to be reserved and quiet because I am a listener. But once I trust someone I am an open. I am playful. People feel at ease around me. With structure and direction, I can achieve anything. I can learn new skills that create a foundation for mastery." She paused. "What do you think so far?"

"I can see resemblance. Tell me the other passage." I replied. I was curious and interested.

"Okay. It says here I possess a relaxed and focused, masterful nature. I have a strong will and can be stubborn at times. Much success in the business world will be a great advantage. This doesn't limit my capacity to be successful in other types of careers, especially if self-chosen and self-driven. When I am relaxed I can be very happy and content, and other people can feel the happiness vicariously. When I am in a happy, healthy relationship I can be my best self for myself, and for my partner. I am a person who mates for life with the right person." She paused again. "What do you think?"

"That does sound like you." I commented. Jenna laughed.

"See? I told you this kind of thing could be fun."

"I didn't say it wasn't." I said. "I still love you. Does it say we're compatible?"

"I love you, too. Let's see if I can find the compatibility passage. Here it is. It says this is a love-at-first-sight combination. High attraction can occur quickly. It endures the test of time. When conflict arises either one of them will make amends. A rupture in the relationship can strengthen the relationship, with conflict resolution. Both signs are willing and capable to resolve conflict, especially with a strong foundation and friendship to bond them. Communication is something both signs can improve on, and this can enhance all parts of their relationship. Above all, the loving, giving, and playful nature of both signs make a relationship deep, meaningful, and can survive long-term. Having common goals while appreciating each other's differences and similarities is a positive attribute to this pairing. These two signs can learn from each other. When in a happy, healthy relationship they can inspire and grow while being together, making this a possible great match all around."

"That sounds beautiful. I hope that applies to us."

"I think it does. We've come this far haven't we my love?"

"Indeed. I love you, Jenna."

"I love you, too, Sakura."

I turned on the radio and we listened to all sorts of songs from the present and a few old ones. We sang and danced. It was so much fun being with her. I wanted our fun times to never end.

We reached Emi's cabin late that evening. Jenna and I packed soup and Chinese food, which we consumed right after we arrived. I dressed in my pajamas and joined Jenna at the fireplace. It was pouring rain outside, and it was cold. I handed her a cup of hot cocoa.

"Thank you, babe," she said. She was wearing her sexy, black, lacy dress wear that looked like a mini dress. It reached down to her knees.

"You're welcome honey." I sipped my mug of cocoa and stared at the small, burning fire. I asked if she wanted any marshmallows. She said that she didn't. When we were done with our drinks, we fell asleep in each other's arms on the cozy sofa.

I woke up to find myself in a chamber surrounded by many candles. I was lying on the ground. My head throbbed, and I felt a large bump on the back of my head when I placed my hand on it. Someone in a navy-blue hooded cloak stood in front of me. He turned around and faced me, glowering.

"Do you know why you are here?" he asked me.

"No. Who are you?" I asked.

"I am the ultimate being"

"What do you mean?"

"I am powerful than you'll ever be, Sakura."

"How do you know my name?" I felt scared. He ignored my question.

"Hand over Jenna and no one will get hurt."

"Never." I said bitterly.

"Then you leave me with no choice." The man summoned two of his subjects. They were dressed in black hooded cloaks. They slowly walked up to me and revealed their faces. I recognized that they were Fred Little and Jack Johnson. They both strapped me to a wall. My hands and feet were bind with rope. Fred stripped my clothes off until all was left were my undergarments. Jack stared at me and licked his lips. His eyes turned yellow. Fred looked at Master and nodded his head. He slapped my face. My cheek stung.

"What do you know about us, Sakura?" interrogated Jack.

"I know nothing." I insisted.

"Yes, you do. You hold a dark secret that could destroy us all. Tell us what that is before it's too late. That's what Master wants. Confess!" yelled Fred.

"I don't know!" I said angrily. Fred slapped me again.

"Enough!" bellowed their leader.

"Yes, Master," both men, said in unison.

"Leave her to me," he said. Fred and Jack obeyed and disappeared. I became extremely nervous. I didn't know what to expect from him or how to endure what I was about to face. He slowly removed his hood and revealed his face.

CHAPTER SIXTY

I woke up the next morning to an empty cabin. I panicked. I called for Sakura. I had a sinking feeling that she was kidnapped by The Immortals. Angrily, I stomped to the bathroom mirror, looked my face, closed my eyes and called forth for Master. After much deliberation, he finally responded to my telepathy.

"WHAT?" he said rudely.

"Where is she?"

"WHO?"

"Don't play stupid with me. I know you have her. What have you done with her?"

"OH. HER?" Master sent me a picture image of Sakura through my mind. She was strapped to a wall wearing nothing but her bra and underwear. I was shocked.

"You asshole! How dare you—"

"SHE'S ABSOLUTELY SAFE HERE WITH ME. IF YOU WANT HER, YOU MUST RETURN TO THE TEMPLE. I AM WILLING TO NEGOCIATE WITH YOU THIS TIME."

"How do I know you will keep your word?"

"YOU DON'T HAVE ANY OTHER CHOICE. COME ALONE. WE WILL BE WAITING FOR YOU. ALL OF US."

"Fine. But you better not harm her."

"I HAVE NO GUARANTEES. THE OTHERS ARE FEELING VERY FRUSTERATED AND VERY THIRSTY NOW. I SUGGEST THAT YOU MAKE HASTE. OH, AND JENNA, COME BACK AS YOUR TRUE SELF. GET RID OF THOSE DAMN CONTANCTS AND HAIR DYE. YOU DON'T LOOK VERY GOOD."

"Screw you!"

"LET'S NOT ARGUE AGAIN. IF YOU DON'T DO AS I TELL YOU, SAKURA WILL GET HURT."

"Fine! I'll be there as fast as I can!" I fled out of the cabin and drove to SeaTic Airport. I bought a ticket to Tokyo.

CHAPTER SIXTY-ONE

I stared at the young man dressed in blue. He descended to the ground and walked up towards me. His eyes were dark brown. His face was oval with a light brown complexion. He had long, straight, black hair that reached his shoulders and he had a scar on his left cheek. He was about a year younger than I was. He was my brother.

"Toru? Is that you?" I asked him.

"Indeed, it is, sister," said Toru.

"But why? Why are you doing this?"

"I was born a leader, Sakura. My mother was the former leader of the Immortal Beings, and it was natural that I take over for her as she lives a more normal life with dad. She taught me everything I had to know at a young age. Your father, Kyo was weak. He couldn't keep such a secret and mother shot him when he tried to warn you about it. Then she took her own life." I bared my teeth at him. I had a feeling Hana was responsible for my father's death.

"You're horrible, Toru. Both you and Hana." I said.

"Ha! I'm merely doing my duty as Master. And don't you dare insult my mother again, Sakura. She was never your mom to begin with. Besides, Hana was stronger than Kyo. Always remember that. Kyo was a weakling, just like you. It's a pity that she faded away last year."

"How?" I asked.

"Good try, Sherlock. I'm not going to give away my weakness to someone distrustful as you. Figure it out for yourself."

"It'll save me time if you just tell me." I said.

"Dream on. I won't tell you a thing."

"Don't worry. I will destroy you and everyone will be free of the curse you've had several people contracted.

"Don't put too much hope on that idea, Sakura," he said.

"I will put much faith to the end of your legacy, Toru. Your short legacy." I said.

"Very well. Do as you please. And that look doesn't suit you. Let's get rid of that make over of yours." Toru closed his eyes and stretched his arms out. He started to hum. My hair changed back to its natural color and length. My eye contacts fell out. "There. Much better," he said. Then he sauntered out of the room, leaving me alone and attached the wall.

I hung against the wall unaware of how much time passed. My mouth became dry and I felt thirsty. I was starting to get a headache. Without my clothes I began to feel cold. I started to think no one would ever come and try to rescue me. Just then, a tall, slender woman walked into the room and stood in front of me. Her skin was tanned, her eyes were hazel, and her hair was short, white blonde. She scrutinized me.

"You must be Sakura, correct?" she questioned. She spoke with a thick Australian accent.

"Yes. I am." I said.

"It's nice to finally meet you," she said. "I've been waiting for this day for a long time."

"Who are you?" I asked.

"I'm Jessica."

"Okay." I said.

"Has Jenna told you about me?"

"No, she hasn't."

"That's not nice of her."

"Why do you say that?"

"Because I'm her girlfriend. That's why." Jessica emphasized the word "girlfriend."

"Oh." I said. I felt as if I was stabbed in the gut.

"Listen. I don't know what Jen has told you, but she's mine. You got that? She and I go back a long way, and we never really broke up. She loves me more than she'll ever love you. I don't even know why the bloody hell she would go after someone as dull as you are. She often goes for women better looking." Jessica said bitterly.

"It was a mistake that she dated you." I said coldly.

"I am very pretty. You ugly bitch!"

"You're wrong. Jenna's with me." I said firmly. I refused to believe her.

"Believe it or not, sweetie. Jenna never really cared about you if you thought she did. She was just being with you because she pitied you. It was never for real. Jenna's the type that only date certain women. If not, she goes out for a one-night stand and leaves afterwards. She would never settle with commitment unless it's with me because I'm the type she fancies. Just let it go. The relationship you had with her was shallow. And not worthwhile contemplating anymore. What you had with her was meaningless and nothing to Jenna." I became very irritated and I wasn't in the best mood for arguing with Jessica.

"I bet the only reason she ever got back together with you is so that she could demonstrate how much she has changed as a person. And tell you that you aren't her type." I said.

"That's wrong! She came back because she likes me more." Jessica stuck her tongue out.

"You were probably her last resort." I snorted.

"Shut up! You don't know a thing about Jenna."

"Oh yeah? Try me." I challenged her.

"Fine. What's her favorite dish?"

"Omelet stuffed with cheese, green and red peppers, carrots, and celery."

"When did she lose her virginity?"

"At age seventeen."

"Who are her parents?"

"Elizabeth Smart from Perth and William Watson from Sheffield. She was an only child." Jessica seemed to be getting irritated at my right answers. She really wanted me to answer incorrectly.

"What kind of perfume does she wear?"

"Lavender."

"Shitty." Jessica muttered.

"See. I know my Jenna." I boasted.

"She's mine, you bloody bitch!" She slapped my face.

CHAPTER SIXTY-TWO

I ran out of the airport and got into a taxi when I arrived at Tokyo. The temple was located afar from the city near a large, remote forest. The other Immortals were guarding the entrance. I hid behind some bushes and closely examined their demeanor. Fred and Jack were paired up to guard outside. They were not armed, but I knew they could fight well if they could try. Knowing that Jack couldn't resist sexual temptation, I pulled up a portion of my jeans and exposed my shaven, smooth, radiant leg. I stuck my leg out of the bushes so that only Jack could see it. Knowing that Fred had a short attention span and preferred observing nature, I threw a large rock I found in the undergrowth at his direction as he watched the forest.

Just as I predicted, Fred ran towards to inspect the rock. Jack hurried over to my leg, drooling along the way. Before he could touch me, I kicked him in the crotch and pulled him in the shrubbery. I sealed his mouth and asked him where Master hid Sakura. He told me he hid her the chamber and gave me directions. I thanked him. Then I punched him in the face to knock him out temporarily. Fred hurried over to the bushes to check out what all the noises were. I jumped out and tackled the large man to the ground and rendered him unconscious.

I cautiously walked inside the temple. I followed Jack's directions. I strolled forward, took a right, turned left, and went down the staircase. When I reached the bottom of the stairs, I turned left and found the chamber door being guarded by Jeff and Nick. They were both armed with machetes. I hid behind a wall.

As Nick walked into my direction, I extended my leg to make him trip. He stumbled to the ground as I grabbed his machete and used the unsharpened end to hit him in the head unconscious. Jeff charged towards me when he found out what was happening. I dodged him, and we fought ruthlessly against each other with our weapons. I defeated Jeff a few minutes later. Like the rest, he was knocked out cold temporarily.

I swung the chamber door opened and ran inside. The lights went on and I was disappointed to see Sakura not there. Cindy stood in the middle the empty room. She pointed at the door behind her and told me that Sakura was in there. I thanked her and began running towards it when Cindy motioned me to stop.

"I told you to take good care of her, Jenna. You don't deserve her," said Cindy.

"She was in perfect hands before she was kidnapped!" I snapped.

"I'm sorry, but it's Master's orders. I cannot let you through."

"Come on, Cindy. Be reasonable. Who cares about what Master says? He can't do anything."

"Yes, he can, Jenna," she said coldly. She glared at me. "He will hurt Sakura if you disobey him. I am not going to take such a crazy risk."

"Either way, he will do harm. We have to take drastic action."

"You can do what you want, but I will not let you pass."

"Is there any way to get through?"

"You can pass if you can get through me, Jenna."

"I accept your challenge."

"Put down the machete. Let's fight this with all the skills we have."

"Very well. As you wish." I said confidently.

Cindy and I bowed before we fought. I took the defense as she threw numerous, hard punches and kicks at me. I knew that after this dispute, I was going to have bruises. Once I found the opportunity, I took the offense. I managed to catch her off balanced after kicking her in the face and punching her in the gut. She fell to the ground.

Before I could make my next move, Cindy got up and performed backward flips. I leapt forward and jumped to do an air kick, but she dodged the hit. She managed to hit me on the face. I fell to the ground. Cindy jumped on me. Her entire weight was on my belly. I couldn't breathe. She wrapped her hands around my throat. Remembering what Sakura did to Sally, I launched my hand to poke Cindy's eyes, but she dodged the hit. I felt helpless. I managed to say a few last words.

"I'm sorry Sakura." I cried.

"Huh?" said Cindy. She continued to add pressure on my throat while I spoke.

"I'm so sorry, Sakura. I've failed to save you." Tears rolled down my eyes. Cindy's face grew sad and she released her grip.

"I'm sorry Jenna," she said. "I had no idea that you really cared for her." I sat up and rubbed my neck. Cindy helped me up.

Just then, Jessica ran up from behind Cindy and hit her in the back of the head. Cindy collapsed to the ground, unconscious. I gawked at Jessica.

"Why the bloody hell did you do that for?" I asked her.

"She almost killed you."

"But she stopped!" I snapped.

"I couldn't let her get away with that."

"But she apologized." I stomped my foot on the ground.

"Whatever," she said dismissively. I started walking towards the door behind her.

"I wouldn't go there if I were you," she warned.

"Why?" I inquired.

"There's nothing interesting there."

"I know that Sakura is there."

"What? You'd rather go and see her than stay here with me?"

"Yes."

"I can't believe you!"

"Well, now you can."

"Jenna, I'm tired of feeling as if I'm in second place."

"I'm sorry to hear that." I said sarcastically.

"You better choose right now. Who do you like more? Me or her?"

"Her." I said firmly.

"Excuse me?"

"You heard me. I don't have to repeat myself." I walked passed her. Jessica stood there frozen. She ran after me and pinned me to the ground. I told her to let me go.

"No." she said stubbornly. "If I can't have you, no one will. I won't let that Sakura take you away from me." She kissed me deeply and started unbuttoning my pants. I broke the kiss and started to push her off me.

"Sakura didn't steal me from you, Jess. I was the one who decided to stay with her. I love her. It was my choice. We broke up. Remember? Now get over it! You need to move on."

Jessica's face grew red with fury. I finally succeeded in pushing her off me. I hit her on the head, not very hard. It was just enough to cause her to fall into a sleeping state.

CHAPTER SIXTY-THREE

It was a few minutes after Jessica left when the chamber door swung open and Jenna appeared.

"Jenna!" I was so happy to see her.

"Oh my god, Sakura!" She ran over and untied me from the wall.

"I knew you would come and save me." I said and ran to her to hug her.

"I'm glad you're okay." We hugged each other tightly. Just then, we heard clapping from the distance.

"Well done, Jenna. You passed the test."

"What test?" she asked.

"You knocked out every one of those pathetic Immortals. You're stronger than I thought," said Toru.

"Toru," I said. Jenna looked at me, her mouth wide open.

"You know him?" she asked.

"Yeah. He's my brother."

"Unbelievable," said Jenna.

"That's right, Jenna. I'm Toru Kawasaki, Sakura's brother by marriage of my mother with her father when they were both alive."

"What do you want?" yelled Jenna.

"Now's the time. My time will soon end, and it will be your time to take over, Jenna."

"I don't want to take over."

"You have no choice. Now, for your final mission, Jenna." Toru closed his eyes and rubbed his temples with his fingers.

CHAPTER SIXTY-FOUR

"What do you want, Toru?" I asked.

"IT'S MASTER!"

"Whatever."

"YOU CAN TAKE OVER IF YOU KILL SAKURA. THAT'S YOUR FINAL MISSION, JENNA."

"Do you really expect me to do that? Hell fucking no!"

"DON'T ATTEMPT TO DEFY ME!!!"

Toru opened his eyes and hovered over to Jenna. His hands landed on Jenna's throat. Sakura ran over and started hitting his back with her fists and then her feet by kicking. Toru laughed and punched his sister so hard that Sakura flew into the air and landed on her back. I bit Toru's arm and kicked him in the crotch. Toru winced and groaned in pain, releasing his grip. I ran over to Sakura and held her up.

"Baby, are you okay?" I asked.

"Yeah. I'm fine. I'm sorry. I don't know what his weakness is."

"It's okay. I'm sure we'll manage somehow. Never lose hope, honey."

"I am very disgusted, Jenna," said Toru. "You have fallen in love with an average human being. The rules are to only perform courtship among fellow Immortals."

"Screw the rules. And I am not a member of this stupid clan anymore. I bet I'm not Immortal either. You're just controlling me!" I said.

Toru started vibrating and levitating higher with his eyes closed. I suddenly felt famished and dehydrated. I yearned for blood.

"NOW'S YOUR LAST CHANCE. BITE HER." I cringed and crinkled my face, trying to ignore the order.

"Sweetie, what's wrong?" Sakura asked.

"No! I won't bite her!" I barked.

"YOU CAN NOT STOP ME!"
"Yes, I can. If you're alive, I can end your life!"
"YOU FOOL! I'M INVINCIBLE! I CAN'T BE DESTROYED!"
"Liar!"

CHAPTER SIXTY-FIVE

I couldn't stand what Jenna was going through. It looked completely painful and horrid for someone to control your mind like that. I didn't want my brother to get away with his actions, either. So, I spoke aloud.

"Toru, this is between you and me."

"What the hell do you want?" he asked snobbishly.

"Set Jenna free."

"What will I get in return?" he asked.

"I will sacrifice myself to you. I will give you my soul."

"Sakura, no!" said Jenna.

"You mean to tell me that you would trade yourself for this weakling?" Toru questioned.

"Yes." I said.

"Good try, sis. Doing noble things won't get you out of this." He laughed. He handed Jenna a knife and whispered in her ear to kill me. I snatched it away from her and noticed the knife was wooden and smelled like garlic. I took a chance and threw it into Toru's heart. Toru collapsed to the ground, groaning. Steam exited from his body and he shook all over. I went over to him and looked at his face.

"So, you finally figured it out," he told me.

"Yes."

"How?"

"Ever since I laid my eyes on you, I knew you feared me the most because I am only human, and it frightened you even more for I was related to you. The only person who can really end this was me because we are family. I was your only sibling in our immediate family. With dad and mom gone, I was your closest family member left who can end it all. No one else can."

"Don't let me die like this. We can conquer the world together."

"Father killed Hana, huh." I needed to know how his mother died.

"Yes."

"How did it happen?"

"Hana was with Kyo in the hospital before he died. And right before he passed, he made the ultimate move. Mom died beside him after he did the same thing that you did to me."

"You went through so much already, Toru. If I don't end it now, you will come back scarred and bitter for as long as you are around. May your sins be forgiven," I began to pray for him.

"No! Stop that."

"It's for your own good. You'll thank me someday."

"I don't need your care! I don't need forgiveness. Give me hatred and the darkness, damn it! I tried to kill your loved one, so you can despise me more! Loathe me! It gives me strength. Don't do what you're doing. I'm growing weak fast." Steam and smoke continued to escape through his body. I continued to pray and ask for forgiveness on behalf of him. To the Universe. Jenna came and joined me.

"May you be forgiven, Toru. May you find your peace," we said in unison. Within minutes, Toru disappeared forever. He left behind his navy-blue cloak. I scooped it up and we burned later it so that no one would ever wear it. The curse was finally over. The people who were part of the clan of Immortals and under Toru's control became mortal again.

CHAPTER SIXTY-SIX

"Are you sure you want to do this?" asked Sakura.

"Yes."

"But it's silly."

"It's the only way to see if it's true." It's been a month since Toru transitioned out of the world. The other Immortals became human again and resumed their lives as if nothing happened at all. They all had permanent amnesia regarding involvement with the clan. Jessica finally got over me and decided to go out with Cindy. Sally was re-arrested by police and convicted of murder for the incident that occurred at Upgate Mall. She spent the rest of her life in prison.

All the members were cured except me. My wounds healed immediately, and I still sometimes had an appetite for blood. I resisted from temptation and was feeling weaker and weaker as each day progressed. I needed to know why I wasn't cured, but I didn't give up on finding the cure. I didn't want to be a Vampire anymore. I wanted to be human.

"Here, love," said Sakura. She handed a cutting knife to me. I made a tiny, superficial cut on my arm. It faded within a minute.

"I don't understand why I'm still Immortal. I don't want to live forever." I felt extremely disappointed.

"Why do you say that?" asked Sakura.

"Because if I do live forever, I will be left behind. When you pass away, I would have to deal with that burden forever. Everyone I meet will progress in life and I would be stuck looking in my early twenties and never feel human. It's interesting because I grew up normally as child and it was until I turned 29 that I stopped aging."

"Hmm. Perhaps…" she began.

"What? What's you're idea?" I was desperate.

"Maybe that's your destiny," she said sadly.

"I don't like it." I said.

"I know. Wait!"

"What?"

"I think I got it!" she said excitedly.

"What?" I repeated.

"I don't know if it will work, but maybe the reason you are still Immortal is because you lack something human."

"Of course. I lack the ability to live a life with an ending."

"No, not just that. You see, I had a dream last night. It wasn't dark or mysterious like my previous dreams. Those are over. This one was hopeful. Because we were bed and we woke up one day knowing we were both human. Jenna, you were human. Just like me. You knew because you no longer had cravings for blood and you could get injured. It just happened. You woke up one day and you're human. No longer a Vampire. Maybe that's what will happen to you. I don't know when, but it's possible. That's what my dream was."

"Babe, I really wish that could come true. It would be my one and only birthday gift to last me the rest of my life. I want nothing more than to spend a single lifetime with you and to age with you."

"Me, too honey. I really do. It's been a month."

"Yes, a long month it's been."

That evening we slept in our bed and held each other tightly. In my mind I wished Jenna was no longer a Vampire. I wished she could be human and live a fair human life. When I fell asleep I had the same dream again. Jenna woke up and realized she was human.

The next morning Jenna and I woke up at the same time. Just like in my dream. I greeted her good morning and kissed her cheek. She then kissed my lips and returned the greeting. She smiled, but then accidentally bit her lower lip hard. Jenna winced, and I asked her if she were okay. She nodded and wiped her lip. It was bleeding.

We waited for a minute for her lip to heal because it took less than a minute for any would to heal up. A minute passed, and her lip was still in the same condition. I pointed out this observation to her. Her eyes widened, and she hurried to the bathroom. She was pleased to see that her lip did not heal right away. Then she took a small knife and made a superficial cut on her arm. She felt stinging pain and waited to see what happened.

The cut did not disappear after several minutes. She grew more excited. At this point I walked over to her and offered to do one more task to see if there were any other changes. I took the small knife and made a small cut on my finger. Enough for it to bleed slightly. I put my finger to her nose and had her smell. Then I placed my finger on her upper lip. She wasn't enticed at all. She reported no cravings or urges for blood, even when my blood was present, which before was never the case.

In fact, she quickly cleaned my wound and put a band aid on it. Then she kissed my finger and smiled. Her lip was still a little bruised, but that didn't matter so much to me. I still kissed her passionately yet careful to not cause pain. I stroked her arm where she made the cut and told her we needed to put on a band aid on that, too. She agreed. She was so happy. She reported it was her first time ever using band aids for real.

"I never felt so…alive."

"That's good. Now you don't have to ever worry about that anymore, Jenna. You're human." I smiled broadly.

"And all I really needed was to be patient and trust your vision dreams. I'm so happy. Thank you, my love." I said and smiled. "It's great to be truly alive!"

I held my darling and embraced her tightly in my arms. She was my blue rose and I was her red rose. We were soulmates. We were lovers and best of friends. We happily lived together in our cozy Sea Town home through ripe age.

THE END

Printed in the United States
By Bookmasters